KU-488-417

Puffin Plus

A Midsummer Night's Death

Since his kidnapping and shooting in *Prove Yourself a Hero*, Jonathan Meredith thought that he had had enough excitement to last him a lifetime. Now back at school, he is once again swept into difficulties far beyond his control.

Standing at the window of his study, Jonathan was amazed to see the police cars on the gravel below. It was a perfect summer morning, wasted by having to be spent on deadly school work.

But the cars heralded a really dramatic piece of news: the body of the unpopular English master, Mr Robinson, had been taken from the river early that morning. Some of Jonathan's friends reacted badly to the news, but Jonathan himself wasn't really affected, and any concern he might have felt was quickly wiped from his mind when another master, Charles Hugo, invited him to join a climbing expedition in Wales.

Jonathan's deep admiration for Hugo made him a little uneasy, for he had to admit it came close to hero worship. But Hugo really *was* admirable, Jonathan told himself, not only as a famous mountaineer, but as a man of great self-knowledge and control. So it was very disturbing to discover that Hugo had told the police he hadn't seen Robinson the evening before his death – because Jonathan knew it was a lie. He didn't really want to think about it, but circumstances were to make it impossible to forget . . .

K.M. Peyton is the author of the *Flambards* books. Like *Flambards*, *A Midsummer Night's Death* is an absorbing piece of story-telling, full of mystery and excitement.

A MIDSUMMER

Puffin Books

K.M.PEYTON

NIGHT'S DEATH

in association with Oxford University Press

Puffin Books, Penguin Books Ltd, Harmondsworth, Middlesex, England
Penguin Books, 625 Madison Avenue, New York, New York 10022, U.S.A.
Penguin Books, Australia Ltd, Ringwood, Victoria, Australia
Penguin Books Canada Ltd, 2801 John Street, Markham, Ontario, Canada L3R 1B4
Penguin Books (N.Z.) Ltd, 182-190 Wairau Road, Auckland 10, New Zealand

First published by Oxford University Press 1978
Published in Puffin Books 1981

Copyright © K.M. Peyton, 1978
All rights reserved

Set in Kuala Lumpur
Printed in Great Britain by
Cox & Wyman Ltd, Reading
Set in Paladium Medium

Except in the United States of America,
this book is sold subject to the condition
that it shall not, by way of trade or otherwise,
be lent, re-sold, hired out, or otherwise circulated
without the publisher's prior consent in any form of
binding or cover other than that in which it is
published and without a similar condition
including this condition being imposed
on the subsequent purchaser

TO JOY

CHAPTER
1

'Dear Mother and Dad,' Jonathan wrote, 'Duty letter coming up, as per school rules. As missives from this foolishly trusting school are not subject to censorship, I might as well use up my two sides by commenting on what a dump it is. Truly the place is full of nutters, and I don't mean the pupils. Think of all the lovely money you would save if you took me away and sent me to the home comprehensive. They are taking girls in the sixth form here now which, considering the closeness of the community and the progressiveness of the famous atmosphere (joke), might prove dangerous.'

'Really,' said Mrs Meredith to her husband. 'Have you read this letter of Jonathan's? He does write very peculiar letters.'

'Not yet.'

'Did you know Meddington was taking girls?'

'No. But I'm not surprised. Single-sex establishments are on the decline.'

'He says the place is full of nutters. His word.'

'Well, boarding-schools these days tend to get a lot of children from broken homes. It solves what to do with them, for term-time, at least. Thank goodness Jonathan doesn't come into that category.'

'Don't sound so self-satisfied, James. He implies that the teachers are nutters, as he puts it, not the pupils.'

'As the Meddington policy is to appoint teachers who have made their mark in the world in other spheres, it follows that they might possibly be unusual. Perhaps that's what he means. Like that maths chap, Hugo – climbed in one of the Everest expeditions, didn't he? Must be a bit out of the ordinary, chap who's done that.'

'Stop talking like the school prospectus. I don't find Jonathan's letters at all encouraging – apart from the fact that he can write proper English. Considering how much the place costs us, I would wish that the content was a little more amenable. He certainly doesn't seem to appreciate his fortune in being there. Are you having another cup of coffee before you go?'

'No, dear. It's gone seven-thirty. I must dash. Give me Jonathan's letter. I'll read it in the train. And don't worry about him – nutters indeed! The atmosphere in that place is thoroughly wholesome, most impressive. That's his trouble perhaps – too degenerate to appreciate its value. I only wish I'd had his opportunities when I was a boy.'

'Yes, dear. Have you got your reading glasses? Gloves? And take an umbrella. It looks changeable.'

They pecked dutifully and Mr Meredith drove in his new Rover to the nearest mainline station and caught a train to London. Settling in his first-class compartment, he first read Jonathan's letter, smiling a trifle grimly, then quickly ran his eyes over the front page news of *The Times* before turning to the business pages. A headline half-way down caught his eyes.

'Tragedy at famous school'.

The name Meddington sprang out as if in coloured print, jangling his complacency.

'Good God,' he said out loud.

The date on the paper was the twenty-first of June. He pulled Jonathan's letter out of his pocket again.

'"Truly this place is full of nutters, and I don't mean the pupils."' The letter was dated the nineteenth.

'Good heavens!' Pursing his lips, Mr Meredith read the piece of news through to the end, then sat, the business pages forgotten, staring out of the window at the flying landscape.

Jonathan, standing in his pyjamas at the window of his study, was amazed to see the police cars on the gravel below. It was only seven o'clock, much too early for anything but emergencies. Such as . . .? he pondered. Burglary, sudden death, murder – the possibilities were intriguing. He raised the sash and leaned out over the stone sill, assessing the situation.

It was a perfect morning, the grounds of Meddington at that hour lying pure and unsullied from horrid child. Acres of perfect grass mowed in curving stripes led the contemplative eye past the magnificent specimen trees and shrubberies to the river and the enormous, trembling tents of the willows, green-gold against misty banks like a Monet painting. Jonathan half-expected to see his own footsteps still in the dew, his secret path printed from the night before. But there were no clues. Wood-pigeons crooned softly from the arboretum, and the scent of the pines was sharp, the smell of early morning drawn out by the dampness of the dew, delicious and provocative. Wasted, Jonathan thought, hating Meddington, and seeing nothing ahead of him but maths etc. and an economics lecture, a prefects' meeting and deadly cricket. The early morning promised everything, but fulfilment was doomed. Life is not for this, Jonathan thought. But the police cars made him feel better.

'Ashworth, you grampus,' he addressed his slumbering room-mate. 'The fuzz is below. Or, the fuzz are below.' He considered it, and put his foot against Ashworth's rear, shaking it to life. 'The fuzz is here. Come and look.'

'What d'you mean?'

'Police. One car parked immediately below. One outside the front door. And goings-on down by the river. Uniformed men searching river-bank.'

Movements under the curtains of the willows had caught his eye and he fetched his binoculars from a cupboard. A houseboat was moored there, the home of Robinson, one of the English teachers. A policeman was standing on the deck, talking to another on the bank.

'They're on Robinson's boat. Perhaps his wife has murdered him.'

'Perhaps he's committed suicide,' Ashworth said. 'After yesterday I wouldn't blame him.'

'What happened yesterday?'

'We upset him, to put it mildly. He ran out of the room screaming. Mostly my fault.'

Robinson, appointed for his prowess in the world of poetry rather than for strength of character, was notoriously unable to control a class. Even the sixth form played him up, having little sympathy for his conceits.

'Really? Well, that's where it's all happening. Enter Mrs Robinson, left, weeping.'

He steadied the binoculars on the window-sill, focusing more accurately. 'By George, she is too. Weeping, I mean. Policeman lending large handkerchief.'

'Are you serious?' Ashworth sat up in bed, bleary but worried. 'You aren't making it up?'

'No. Definitely our Patsy weeping. What do you think has happened?'

'He was in a terrific bate – Robin was, I mean. Quite enough to throw himself in.'

'We'd have known before now, surely? This was four o'clockish, yesterday, I take it? Your guilty conscience is at work. Perhaps she's just dropped something in, her diamond necklace or something.'

But Patsy wasn't the diamond necklace sort, and that would hardly warrant two cars at seven a.m. Ashworth joined Jonathan at the window, blinking. He was a

10

thick, pudgy youth whose company Jonathan bore with fortitude, having been parted from his volatile friend Macey, initially for punishment and lately (and more decisively) by Macey's having left school to join the Navy. Jonathan missed Macey and hadn't found anyone to take his place. Ashworth was just an oaf. His oafish face was now working with self-pity.

'You don't really think –? He wouldn't, would he, just because of me?'

'Wouldn't what?'

'Drown himself.'

'Who said, you idiot? As if anyone would, for you!' Jonathan's voice grated with scorn and despair. He saw the look on Ashworth's face and softened. 'He was alive and well last night at ten o'clock, if that's any consolation. I saw him on the boat, talking to Mr Hugo.'

'How come? What were you doing down there at ten o'clock? It's out of bounds.'

Ashworth, if he had looked carefully, would have seen a slight colour touch Jonathan's cheeks. But Jonathan said, 'That's all I'm saying,' and turned away from the window rather abruptly. There were some things hard to admit even to oneself and Jonathan certainly would not admit to as dire a being as Ashworth that he had followed Mr Hugo down to the river on the offchance that he might – might – and here it was, even in his mind, this uneasy guilt when it came to the strange private feeling he had for Hugo, as if it were something wrong. It wasn't as if he wasn't perfectly normal in liking girls; it was just that one didn't admit to the sort of feeling he had for Hugo, not to anyone else, at least. Macey had known, but it had been a private thing, even then. Once it had been the decent thing for a boy to hero-worship the athletics master; most jolly schoolboy books had been full of blatant admissions of admiration and reverence. But now it wasn't the in-thing at all. It was modish to despise the whole wretched race, and keep one's professed admiration for spotty rock stars and eccentric footballers. But ever since Charles Hugo had arrived at the school, wreathed in public acclaim already for his feats in the Himalayas, Jonathan had taken an instinctive liking to his quiet authority, his cool, rather distant, personality and dry humour. Unlike Robinson the poet, Hugo never had the slightest difficulty in keeping order and exacting respect. Everyone liked him. But in Jonathan's case it was liking exaggerated into – well, what? Jonathan asked himself defensively. And yes, he was forced to admit, he supposed it went too far, for the admiration was completely without criticism. To Jonathan Hugo could do no wrong. Hugo was wisdom and justice personified, courage and endurance made flesh. So what if I admire him, Jonathan thought? He is more admirable in every way than any person I have ever come across. Yet he felt he had to justify it – which was all so stupid, to feel that one must justify a feeling so instinctive and satisfying. Perhaps it was the unnaturalness of being enclosed in the Meddington monasterial setting that made quite natural feelings suspect. Five hundred odd hothouse boys deep in a charmed countryside, enclosed by a high wall and the splendid plantings of past century parkmakers, could hardly be considered as other than a lopsided community, unhealthily privileged in some spheres and shockingly deprived in others. The cautious infiltration of the sixth-form girls was a pathetic gesture. There were about a dozen of them and they contributed about as much glamour as the sheep used to keep down the grass on the football pitch. They were either poised and arrogant and frankly terrifying, or giggly and fluffy and secretive; one, called Iris Webster, was quite obviously a lunatic, imported for her musical talent, admittedly formidable, but given to ankle-length dresses of Indian cotton and hair the colour of old hay right down past her bottom. All this when sixth-form boys, in spite of a supposed progressiveness, had to wear ties, white shirts and dark trousers for lessons, no doubt to

12

acclimatize them to the decades that stretched ahead in the offices of industry and commerce.

'Oh, jeez!' he groaned, seeing the day ahead, the weeks till the end of term, and a whole year after that until release. He felt much too old to be at school. The thing about Hugo was just a bypath to relieve the boredom. He never gave him a thought in the holidays.

Having got out of bed there wasn't much point in going back, so he washed and dressed. By breakfast time there was a distinct unease in the atmosphere, the police presence having made itself felt. Jonathan, trailing down the wide carved staircase into the Victorian Gothic hall, saw the Head talking to a stranger at the door of his office. He looked shaken and pale. It was quite noticeable, not just an imagined change in demeanour. The Head, Armstrong, was normally a pretty relaxed fellow, not – thank God – given to tyranny or pomp, but he now looked far from relaxed. The stranger went into the office with him and the door shut. Scotland Yard, Jonathan thought. Drug squad superintendent. C.I.D. Forensic expert. Life was looking up.

Jonathan breakfasted at the prefects' table as usual, on sausages and tomatoes, toast and marmalade and strong tea. He had been made a prefect against his will. ('You can't shelve your responsibilities in this life, Meredith, I'm afraid. Would that we could all sit back and observe, as seems to be your way, rather than shoulder the burden.' What utter drivel, thought Meredith, seeing as most of his contemporaries couldn't wait to get into positions of power and shoulder the burden of keeping lesser mortals in their lowly places. It wasn't a role that appealed to him at all, although he had no difficulty in carrying it out, a lot less in fact than most of his fellow despots.)

Surmise on the police presence was the sole topic of conversation.

'Can't be burglary, seeing as what there's nothing of value in the old pile save Maggie's electric typewriter.'

'They're after the druggies, what do you bet? They'll be rifling our dorms this very minute.' A few experimental dope smokers looked worried to death at this, and several sausages were pushed miserably aside.

Jonathan noticed that Robinson wasn't at breakfast, but this fact wasn't significant, as Robinson often wasn't at breakfast, being a lazy sod who couldn't get up in the mornings. The rest of the staff were distinctly quieter than usual. Watching, Jonathan decided that they were all shocked by whatever it was that had happened, showing exactly the same symptoms as the Head. The conversation was muted. Hearty Fletcher, Jonathan's house-master, was markedly less hearty than usual, his booming guffaw quelled, his amiable expression puckered into dismay. Linda Slater (music) looked as if she had been crying. Only Charles Hugo looked the same as usual, but as he was generally quiet and grave his normal expression was in keeping. He ate heartily and retired behind *The Times* over a third cup of tea. Death, Jonathan decided. No less. He didn't say this. He sat back, having finished, and his eyes went to the long windows that gave on to the gravel drive. Far away across the lawns the willows wept over the now deserted houseboat. A squirrel ran across the grass. Two policemen walked up from the river. Jonathan sighed.

Meddington school was housed in a rambling Victorian mansion with medieval intentions, the exterior now largely clothed in ivy, the interior lofty, noble and excruciatingly cold in winter. In summer it was quite civilized and Jonathan liked the eccentricity of its towers, buttresses, winding staircases and stone-flagged halls. On some of the knobbly façades, the ivy stripped away, Hugo taught rock-climbing; in one of the towers the music maestros practised through long summer evenings to the accompaniment of nesting swallows and

14

mating cuckoos, and in a baronial dining-room the spasmodic clicking of billiard balls and ping-pong echoed in the hammer-beam. A large, ornate orangery had been converted – in the nineteen-thirties – into a swimming pool, and crouched blue and enticing beneath a wild tangle of passion-flower swinging jungle-wise across the glass roof. Decorated with mosaic floors in the Roman style and smelling to Jonathan strongly of the old Empire, one somehow expected servants to appear with trays of drinks and dry towels. (The river, deep, swift and treacherous, was severely out of bounds for swimming.) The old place had its felicities, but Jonathan always had the feeling that it wasn't part of the real world at all. The police, for instance, looked thoroughly out of place.

More so in assembly.

'We're going to find out,' Ashworth said to Jonathan, taking the seat next to him. 'They're going to tell us'.

The stranger who had been talking to the Head was sitting on the platform. The Head was conferring with him, very strained. The school, piling into the hall, was nervously expectant; a subdued hum of conversation covered every prophecy from the sublime to the ridiculous. Jonathan didn't want to discuss it, not responding to Ashworth who looked worried, nor smiling at Jane Reeves who pushed in beside him – one of the aggressive variety, muscly bare legs stretched out beside his demurely dark trousers, the feet thrust into almost non-existent sandals with toenails painted a violent crimson. On her other side Iris Webster subsided in her clouds of drapery with a jangle of bracelets – no flesh showing there with a vengeance. They really were an extraordinary crew, Jonathan decided, with a sharp pang of regret for the gorgeous Melissa Jones, a hard-riding blonde at home whom he was only free to woo in the holidays. Roll on the holidays!

'Oh, jeez, you don't think it's dope, do you?' Ashworth whispered, having practised it once behind the folly in the arboretum and been violently sick for his trouble. 'Smithers says –'

'No, idiot. Shut up.'

'Smithers says –'

'Shut up!'

'Oh jeez,' said Ashworth.

When everyone had arrived the Head Master moved over to his lectern and silence fell immediately.

'We are not holding a normal assembly this morning.' Armstrong's voice echoed in its usual grotesque fashion round the intricate mouldings of the hall ceiling high above, as if issuing from a deep cave. An acute silence waited on every syllable. 'I have some very grave news to impart, and I think it would be more practical afterwards if we all disperse to lessons immediately.' He paused and glanced at the man sitting at the table behind him. 'With me here on the platform is Detective-Inspector Allen from Thorntonhill. His business here this morning is to make inquiries into the shocking and very sad sudden death of our member of staff, Mr Robinson.'

A tremor of shock moved over the gathering, a sudden hissing and squeaking of excitement, instantly suppressed by Armstrong's upraised hand. Jonathan felt an urgent nudge in his side from Ashworth but declined to acknowledge it. He had not moved, and felt no surprise at the announcement.

The Head continued, 'Mr Robinson's body was taken from the river at the weir at Thorntonhill early this morning. I want to make it clear to you that foul play is not suspected. It appears that he left a letter indicating his intentions, and one would assume that he – he took his own life.' Armstrong cleared his throat, clearly embarrassed by the weight of his news. He glanced at the Detective-Inspector to see that he wasn't saying the wrong things and added, 'All we want to say to you at this stage is that, if anyone knows of any reason why Mr Robinson should have – have felt inclined to do this

16

– this terrible thing – if anyone of you had conversation with him yesterday after lessons, we would like you to tell us. We should also like to speak to the sixth-form English group which he took last period yesterday afternoon. They will know who they are. I would like them to come straight to my study from the hall. And anyone else at all, who thinks they might know of anything which might shed light on –'

At this point in the speech Jonathan, already aware of Ashworth's growing consternation at his side, was unexpectedly distracted by a squeak from Jane Reeves and the sight of Iris Webster falling in a dead faint on the floor – or, at least, sideways over Jane's lap in a flowing disarray of hair and necklaces.

'Oh, help!' Jane said, not the slightest bit of help herself, and Jonathan was forced to get to his feet and get his hands under the collapsed girl's arms and hold her up while Jane wriggled out from underneath. The girl, thin as a stick, seemed to weigh nothing at all.

'If you take her feet we can get her out,' Jonathan said, seeing that he was lumbered. He could easily have lifted her up and carried her, but didn't see why pushy Jane shouldn't do her bit too.

Amongst a great local consternation, gaspings and scrapings of chairlegs they effected their ridiculous retreat to the nearest door and laid Iris out on the floor outside. Mrs Arthurs, a formidable ex-England hockey captain and biology specialist, followed them out and said, 'It's no good leaving her there. She'll have to go into the first-aid room. Can you carry her, Meredith? She's a poor little sparrow. I'm sure it's not beyond your capabilities.'

So much for women's lib., Jonathan thought, staggering up the stairs with Iris Webster in his arms. The two females leading the way had more beef between them than he'd ever have, biceps like trapeze artists. Some sparrow, he thought, after three flights and two long corridors, and dumped his burden unceremoniously upon the sick-room couch. She lay in a pathetic heap, not stirring. Jonathan stood, getting his breath back.

Mrs Arthurs said, 'Stay with her a minute. I'll go and get some water.'

She went out.

Jane said, 'Poor Iris! She'll go potty over this. She's madly in love with him.'

'In love with – ?' Jonathan couldn't believe it. 'You mean with – Robinson?'

'Yes.'

'Good God!' Jonathan tried to imagine anyone loving Robinson, and failed. Even Patsy had given no indication of loving him, usually treating him with the indifference Jonathan always thought he deserved. He was, had been (he conceded) handsome in his weak, effeminate way but –

'I wouldn't have thought it possible,' he said, wondering if these girls were even more peculiar than he had thought. Iris, lying on the bed in her strange gold and green dress, with her hair lying in great loops, hay-gold over the white sheets, looked like a princess out of Grimms' bewitched by a frog-prince. She looked faintly froggy, perhaps the colour, her skin very pale and cold and greenish, her face gaunt and sad. He stared at her in wonder, and then pity. She opened her eyes and looked at him. Her eyes were green-gold like her hair, pale and clear. They fixed on him. He was embarrassed.

'O.K.?' How could she be? Impossible. Silent tears welled up and spilled down on either side of her face.

He looked at Jane and said hastily, 'Woman's work. I've done my bit.'

Jane sighed.

He left and made for his form-room, aware by the noise from below that assembly was over. Just outside the door Ashworth was waiting for him, as wan as Iris but not, so far, in tears.

'Cripes, Meredith, I had to see you first! What shall I do?'

'What do you mean?' Still pondering on the enormity of Iris loving Robinson, Jonathan had overlooked Ashworth's dilemma.

'He did commit suicide, for heaven's sake! I was just joking when I said – but it's true! It was me that got him raving yesterday. They are going to say it was my fault!'

'Listen, twit. You got him raving at four. He certainly wasn't raving at ten, when I saw him. He was lying in a deckchair smoking a fag.'

'Can I say that?'

'God Almighty, no!' Jonathan, for the first time, saw the complications of the case. He grasped Ashworth urgently by the arm. 'On no account say I was down there and saw him. Hugo was with him. He'll say it. You don't want to go blabbing that I said I saw him.'

'Did you?' Ashworth asked, looking curious and suspicious.

Jonathan wished he hadn't said, but as he had he now impressed upon Ashworth, slowly and heavily (for Ashworth was an idiot), 'Yes, but – on – no – account – say so. Not to *anybody* at all.'

'All right.'

Easily led, Ashworth. Jonathan watched him lumber off to the Head's office, and wondered about Hugo being with Robinson, in view of what had happened. But then, no one was to blame for suicide, not directly. There would be an inquest and the reason would be decided and made public and they would all forget about it. For himself, Jonathan wasn't going into mourning. He could easily dispense with Robinson in his life. Hugo now – that might have got him reeling for a moment. The thought of it made him feel quite cold. But then of course Hugo wouldn't do such a damn-fool thing. Funny though, that he was down there last night, in view of what had happened. He might know more about Robinson's motives than anybody else. Which brought him back to where he had started . . . *blast*, for having let Ashworth know what he had seen last night.

'Who's that boy?' Iris asked Jane.

'Name of Meredith. Don't you know? Aren't you in any lessons with him?'

'No.'

'He's maths and law and suchlike agonies. I suppose if you're all music and dance you won't meet. He had to carry you all the way here from the hall. Mrs Arthurs's instructions.'

Iris flushed painfully.

'I'm all right now. You can go if you like.'

'O.K. But Mrs Arthurs says you're to stay here for a bit. You've got everything you want?'

'Yes.'

Jane went. Thank goodness, Iris thought. She didn't want company. She curled up, pulling the blanket over her to make a cave from the unsympathetic sunshine and shut out the blackbird's voice from the ivy. She didn't want to think about what Mr Armstrong had said, only pretend it wasn't true and go on fantasizing in her mind about dear Robin. It had always been fantasizing anyway, only there had always been the real Robin every day to look at, feed upon, and now there wouldn't be. Just a dream, like everything in her life that gave her any joy. Nothing real had ever made her happy yet, not where people were concerned. She had had hopes of Meddington, but she should have known . . . the girls were so sure of themselves, hard and bitchy, and the boys . . . the boys didn't count. They were just little boys, even the ones due to leave. At home there was nothing either, just a London flat and her mother practising, practising . . . trailing to Paris or Amsterdam for a concert, the damned cello travelling as a person and always getting hung up in airline procedure and her mother angry and imperious . . . 'Do you know who I am?' Iris wanted to die every time. It was awful having a mother like that. Her mother's career didn't allow for children. Iris had got used to being seen and not heard, not being any trouble, hardly *being* at all. It had been hard coming to Meddington, to start being some one. Impossible. People had tried with her at first, being kindly, but because she hadn't known how to respond they had got bored. 'You have to give *something*,' Jane had once said. 'However little. For the other person to latch on to. But if you give *nothing* –' (great scorn) – 'you can't expect the other person to do *all* the work.' Well, it made sense, but Iris hadn't particularly wanted to give Jane anything to latch on to.

Once, out of pure shock, she had given Robin something to latch on to, and he had latched and she had fallen in love with him. Just the once. It hadn't continued, for afterwards – well, it was obvious – the only emotion on his side had been frightful embarrassment.

She had gone back for something she had forgotten into a classroom where Robin had just dismissed his contemptuous class, and found him crying. He had been standing in the long bay window, his hands in his pockets, just looking out, quite silent, only with tears running down his cheeks. Although still in his twenties, he was quite a famous poet, much lauded in the Sunday papers (the ones her mother took) and Iris knew that poets were by nature sensitive and given to emotion, so she did not consider it completely unexpected, knowing how he suffered in his classes (if it had been someone like Mr Hugo, for example, one would just not have believed it, put it down to conjunctivitis). But with Robin it seemed a fairly logical reaction and, although shocked, or, perhaps, because shocked, she went over to him, instead of fleeing in horror, and said, 'Can I help you?'

When she thought of her action afterwards, she could not credit it.

He had hitched his seat on a table and said, 'No. No one can help at all, but it's kind of you to ask.'

He had stopped crying though, wiping his face on the back of his sleeve. He had even smiled at her. He had a very thin, haunted-looking face, pale and freckled, with beautiful arching nostrils. He was tall and looked delicate, the wrists and hands bony and frail, the neck fine. He looked like a poet and acted like a poet, appearing at times to inhabit a different plane from his humble classes, which is why his humble classes didn't like him. Opinion differed as to whether he put it on or whether it was real. As it caused so much unhappiness all round Iris supposed it was real.

'I'm no teacher,' he said to her simply. 'I hate this place. I thought I would be able to do it – here, of all places, where it is so beautiful, and they invited me. I don't make much money at poetry, I'm afraid – one doesn't. I thought it would all work out to all our advantages, but I was wrong.'

'It might get better, in time,' she said.

'No time is soon enough,' he said.

What on earth had she looked like, standing there like a scarecrow staring at him? He had looked at her carefully, not unseeing at all, and she had stared back (how could she!) and seen that his eyes were pale with large black irises (drugs?) and that his eyelashes were dark and long, like a girl's, although his hair was blond. She had fallen in love with him at that moment.

He had smiled again and said, 'You, perhaps, of them all, might understand a little bit –'

What had he meant by that? She had thought and thought. Did he think she was – different? She thought that he thought *he* was different.

'You are like Ophelia,' he said.

But Ophelia was mad, Iris remembered. What was the answer to that? Her real nature was taking over, unable to give any more. She remembered she had felt her lips moving, and no words coming out. Robin had stood up and put out his hand and touched her shoulder. When she thought of it, under the blanket, she quivered.

'Don't be unhappy, Iris,' he had said. 'Being gifted is very dangerous. It doesn't make for happiness.'

22

And he had walked out of the room, leaving her gaping like a codfish. The next time he had seen her he had flushed, and then been brisk and slightly sarcastic, which she had put down as a cover-up. He was often like that. His classes didn't like his sarcasm.

'He's so wet, thinking he's a genius all the time,' the boys said disgustedly.

But the critics in the Sunday papers seemed to think he *was* a genius. No one at Meddington thought so.

Iris cried a bit, remembering all this. It didn't surprise her that he had committed suicide. She wondered if she ought to go and volunteer to the Detective-Inspector that she knew Mr Robinson was unhappy and that he had cried that day, and why, but she knew she never would. She lay thinking about him, the tears coming every now and then, yet – very strangely – she knew she wasn't entirely unhappy. There was a sort of satisfaction in what she was doing, isolated, grieving for the beautiful poet, listening to the birds singing.

And, very strangely, for some reason she kept seeing the face of the boy Meredith, when she had come to, and the way he had been looking at her. For all that his eyes were plain common blue with perfectly normal eyelashes, there had been a look in them that she had never discerned in Robin's, for all he was a poet. They had been full of – was she mistaken? – not scorn or exasperation, like Jane's, but compassion. And because sympathy so rarely came her way, Iris remembered it with gratitude. Meredith might be worth knowing.

Meredith, if he had known, would have run a mile. But he was doing maths with Mr Hugo.

Ashworth was trying to explain the disastrous nature of Robinson's last lesson to the Detective-Inspector without getting himself into trouble, but it was impossible.

'I think,' said the Detective-Inspector, 'you had better be utterly clear upon this point: no blame is attached to you for Mr Robinson's death. However ghastly you might have been, and however you might, unwittingly, have added a straw to a disturbed state of mind, by no conceivable stretch of the imagination can the blame be attached to you. So tell me the story plainly, exactly what happened. We have evidence, you see, that he returned to the staff-room from his lesson with you in a very distraught condition.'

'Oh, jeez,' Ashworth thought, rolling his eyes in desperation. Ten other boys stood beside him, equally distraught, the thickies of the Sixth.

'Well?'

'Perhaps,' said Armstrong, guessing what abysmal confidences were about to be revealed, 'they will be more forthcoming if I go next door and dictate a few letters to Miss Anderson? Just call me when you've finished.'

'Very well.'

He departed.

'We were reading *A Midsummer Night's Dream*,' Ashworth mumbled.

It was awful, being compelled to recall what would have been far better, in any circumstances, forgotten. Recited baldly, how could it sound anything but infantile? One could only state facts; it was beyond Ashworth to recall the atmosphere, the last lesson of the long, hot day, through the open windows the distant purring of the mower fading down towards the river and presently returning, a constant, rhythmic summer lullaby, the plopping of tennis balls and the laughing of little boys released early and trailing back to the junior house to get their swimming things. The lumbering mind, summoned, resisted. The heat, the natural inclinations, dulled it beyond hope.

Robin had said, 'Shakespeare has, of course, given nourishment to all manner of men for the last three hun-

24

dred years. Perhaps, given the will, some glimmer of the reason why should penetrate the heads in this room if they work at it hard enough.'

But there was no will. They had groaned.

'Give out the books.'

Ashworth had doled them out and got tripped up by Dickinson for his pains, crashing his funny-bone agonizingly on a chairback.

'Pick your feet up, boy!' Dickinson reproved him noisily.

Ashworth hit him on the head with one of the books and three acts fell out of the middle of it. Four boys leapt to gather them up and Robin shouted at them, goodwill having died a natural death. Ashworth returned to his desk, giggling. He noticed that it was midsummer's day – the date was scrawled on the board, and he felt obliged to point it out. Robin wasn't particularly grateful.

'It would be too much, I suppose, for the fact to improve your rendering of this work? Who is going to read Puck?'

'Smith,' Kemp said.

The hint was taken by the rest of the class.

'Smith for Puck! Up with Smith!'

Smith stood six foot two and had a bulk to match, and the ponderous movements of an elderly elephant. His bland, witless face broke into a slow smile.

'Smith can't read,' Robin said bitterly.

'Yes, he can,' Kemp said. 'Smith can read. Can't Smith read?'

'Yes,' they all said.

'Slowly,' Ashworth added.

'Smith can read Puck slowly,' Kemp said to Robin. 'That's all right, isn't it? We're not in a hurry, are we?'

'Only for the bell,' Robin said.

'Oh, God,' said Robin, 'Titania, the Queen of the Fairies.'

They all fell about.

'I will read the Queen of the Fairies,' Kemp said, in the appropriate voice, so that they all became hysterical.

The inevitable direction of the afternoon was already established, the manipulation of Robin well in hand, in a manner that happened so habitually that it was more boring than a lesson where one actually had to work. Ashworth was cast as Oberon. Robin, the poet, was bound to despair at his motley class, spotted and dull and unwilling. Fantastically imaginative in his use of words, he had no imagination at all when it came to teaching dull boys to appreciate them. They all knew they were doomed, the boys blaming Robin and Robin blaming the boys. It was a familiar pattern, one from which the only escape was the bell.

Ashworth yawned, sitting in a great flood of golden sunshine, frowning at his lines. The boys behind him were scuffling down on the floor over something – 'I've dropped my pencil, sir. I'm sorry, sir, my chairleg got stuck in a hole in the floor, sir. A mousehole, sir.' Gales of laughter. A roar of rage from Robin and through it all Smith stumbling gamely across the hurdles of print:

'And then the whole quire hold their hips and laugh;
And waxen in their mirth, and sneeze and swear
A merrier hour was never wasted there.'

'Enter Oberon!' Robin called out.

Ashworth, startled, sprang to his feet.

What happened next was as much a surprise to him as it was to Robin, and infinitely more painful. Whoever had been groping about on the floor behind him had apparently, without his being aware of it, tied Ashworth's ankles to his chairlegs with bits of string. When Ashworth made his eager entrance his action was abruptly brought up short by the chair's inability to accompany him. He did a surprised nosedive across the aisle and, unable to save himself, crashed into a neighbouring desk and brought it down on top of him. Fettered by the chair, his own landing was awkward and painful. He was aware of an agonized wrenching of his kneecaps and a cascade of books, great shouts of glee and general uproar from above and, over all, Robin's maniacal fury. Breaking point had been reached. He remembered Robin's face, white and jerking, his voice screaming and bits of Shakespeare raining from his copy as it flew across the room. Ashworth couldn't move, and everybody was too busy laughing to help him. By the time he had moaned and threshed about and bitterly complained enough, the bonds were hacked through with somebody's pen-knife and he scrambled to his feet. Robin had disappeared, and Kemp was standing on Robin's desk shouting, 'I'm the Queen of the Fairies!' Some one threw a football boot at him and at this point the Head Master came in. Ashworth, confused, manoeuvred, got the blame, because the desk was still overturned and he was the cause of it, and Kemp said he had climbed on the teacher's desk to try and keep order.

It was terribly hard to describe all this in retrospect.

At the conclusion of his attempt, Ashworth hung his head in shame.

The Detective-Inspector sat for some time making notes, and then said, 'I've got the gist of it then. You say this sort of thing is quite normal? With Mr Robinson, that is?'

Kemp said, 'It was a bit worse than usual. But we usually played up in his lessons.'

'He couldn't keep order?'

'No.'

'You wouldn't behave like this with any of the other teachers?'

'No.'

'You would say that when Mr Robinson left you, he was more upset than usual, or did he often leave you in that state?'

'I should say it was worse, yesterday. Worse than for a long time.'

'And that was the end of the afternoon and he went back to the staff-room?'

Kemp said, 'I had to go to the staff-room when the bell went, sir, and he was in there then.'

'With other members of the staff?'

'Yes. Mr Hugo was there, and Miss Slater and Mr Fletcher. Several of them.'

'I would like you two' – he gestured to Ashworth and Kemp – 'to stay for a bit. You others can go. There's a chance you might be needed to give evidence at the inquest. But nothing to worry about too much. Just stay around, will you? I'll speak to Mr Armstrong.'

Ashworth and Kemp sat down in chairs against the wall, white and silent and horrified.

At the end of the maths lesson Hugo said to Jonathan, 'There'll be a climbing practice tonight, on the folly. It's your turn, isn't it? Do you want to try the traverse between the two upper windows?'

'Oh, yes please!'

'Seven o'clock then, or as soon after supper as you like. And I was thinking – this trip I promised the six of you, in North Wales – I think we might be able to fit it in after all. I've spoken to Mr Armstrong about it. He said I could take you just before we break up, that makes it about a fortnight from now. Midweek, and I think we'll have to camp. The youth hostels are always full this time of year. But I can get the gear and it'll be handier. Shall I put you down for it?'

'Oh yes! Splendid. I thought it was off – you hadn't said anything.'

'No. The summer term gets so tied up, and then I'm flying to the Himalayas the day after we break up – it's hard to organize everything. But I think we can consider it a certainty now.'

Jonathan's spirits soared at the news, the promise of attempting some real climbs with Hugo the very best treat he could think of. They had been once before, but he hadn't known anything then, and Hugo had spent most of his time with a group of seniors. But now Jonathan was a senior, and one of the best when it came to climbing the folly, and with luck Hugo might take just him on the rope with him, or perhaps him and Murphy. Murphy was pretty good ... Hugo climbed like a fly. He went up a Severe without a hesitation, moving as smoothly as if he were on steps. Jonathan had a book written by the leader of one of the Karakoram climbs, and the author said of Hugo: 'Charles Hugo, one of the leading climbers in Britain today, combines an instinctive mountaineering intelligence with an incredible climbing technique. Slight of frame, yet of immense physical strength, he is able to move up apparently holdless rock with a fluency which in itself is an education to watch.'

Jonathan felt of Hugo that a remote Himalayan mountain-top was his spiritual home. He was an intensely private person and, although perfectly approachable and on amicable terms with all members of the staff, he never gave the impression of needing anybody; he never spoke of himself or his experiences; he rarely gave opinions, or criticized, except in the course of lessons. Jonathan thought of him as a very complete person, a man of great self-knowledge and control. He could not imagine him acting impulsively or excitedly or unfairly. Working with him, either at maths or climbing, was systematic, hard and satisfying; one was stretched and encouraged and led to surprising achievements. Yet teaching was obviously only a means for the climber to fill in gaps between expeditions. He bore the Meddington life stoically, but was a man apart. Jonathan liked this attitude. It matched his own feelings exactly. He had not modelled himself on Hugo but rather was attracted to Hugo by the affinity he sensed. It was very satisfying to find oneself in slightly the same mould as such an admirable man. It gave a nice sense of superiority. Jonathan felt that, like Hugo, he really had a mind above Meddington. Not in the academic department, perhaps . . .

'I do think, Meredith, you will have to do this last bit of work again. I can see the way your mind is working, but you can't expect a nine-to-five examiner to do over-time following the convolutions of your thought pro-cesses. A little more method, please, and not so much inspired invention. This isn't the arts stream, you know.'

Jonathan grinned, appreciating the nice phrasing which would have been a mere detention from anybody else.

'Let me have it again tomorrow – I take it that won't keep you from our appointment on the folly? I can give you another day if so.'

'No. I'll try and cut cricket.'

'Fine. Call for me after supper then, when you're ready.'

Hugo lived alone in what had once been a gardener's cottage, a very small, two-up, two-down flint cottage with a patterned tiled roof and tall chimneys. It looked quaint, backing on to a thick pine coppice half-way down the drive to the main gates: as if a gnome should live there but, once inside the front door, the at-mosphere was decidedly ungnomelike. It was stark and uncompromisingly masculine, a minimum of furniture and cosiness, but an abundance of climbing gear in piles on the floor, a crate of high-protein meat substitute, the aluminium frames of a high altitude box tent, canvas bag full of pitons and karabiners, shelves loaded with climbing books and guides and the walls covered with maps. It was a blissful home to Jonathan's way of think-ing, just as much space as one needed and all used to ad-vantage, no interfering woman's hand cluttering it with cushions and rubbish.

He called at the appointed hour, having changed into jeans and plimsolls, and Hugo shouted from upstairs, 'I shan't be a minute. Help yourself to a rope and a helmet.'

Jonathan did so. Although there was no danger of falling stones on the folly, they wore helmets to get used to the feel of them. Jonathan took one from its perch on a pair of stag's antlers fastened over the doorway into the kitchen, hitched an eighty-foot coil of rope over his shoulder and leaned against the porch, waiting. It was a very hot evening, the shadows only just beginning to stretch out over the gold, baked grass, the resinous smell from the pines so strong that it reminded Jonathan of foreign parts. One half-expected lizards and exotic snakes. But there was a very English blackbird, singing fit to burst, and three pairs of house-martins busy with their nests under the carved eaves. They meant good luck, Jonathan remembered. But Hugo was lucky already; he hardly needed their blessing – unless on the expedition to come, where the risks would be high.

'Only as high as you make them,' Hugo always insisted to them, teaching them the proper use of the rope, the various methods of belaying. 'To assess the risk accurately is an important part of the game.'

There was a small car approaching up the drive from the gates, throwing up a cloud of dust like a stage-coach in a Western. Jonathan recognized it as Robinson's car, presumably driven by Patsy, which gave him a nasty sinking feeling, remembering her fate as opposed to his own present entirely happy and unworried state of mind. He hadn't given much thought to the tragedy all day, pursuing his own business and not overlapping with the police overmuch and with the overwrought Ashworth – happily – not at all, but now it came back to him with a crunch, especially as the car seemed to be slowing down. He felt a quick flush of panic, wondering what on earth one said to cover such unspeakable contingencies.

The car stopped and Patsy put her head out.

'Is Charles there?'

Surprised, Jonathan said, 'Yes, I'll call him,' but at that moment Hugo came out. He went over to the car and Jonathan heard Patsy say, 'It's all right, I just wanted you to know . . .' and then they exchanged a few sentences which Jonathan couldn't hear, and Patsy said, 'Do you want a lift? I'm going up to the school.'

'No, we're going to the folly. It's O.K.'

The car drove on and Hugo turned back to Jonathan and said, 'Got everything? I'm ready now.'

'Yes.'

They set off together, padding silently over the soft pine-needle track that skirted the erstwhile vegetable gardens and passing presently into the thick shade of the great girdle of trees that surrounded the school. It was full of midges, heavy with scent of honeysuckle. Jonathan felt deeply, intoxicatingly content, thinking of the traverse, which was difficult and would scare him, set the old pulses thumping as if the blood had gone thick with terror – Jonathan thrived on such experiences. He desperately wanted to go to Wales and do the real thing again, confident that he was in the best hands in the world. Hugo, as usual, said nothing; in fact seemed preoccupied. Jonathan, coming out of his dream, to be polite, said, 'It's not very nice for Mrs Robinson, what happened.' Worse for her, he thought, the manner of dying , than if he had died of an illness.

'No,' Hugo said. 'A terrible shock.' Then he added quietly, 'A blessed release, all the same.'

Jonathan wasn't quite sure if he had heard correctly.

'Who for?'

'Her, of course.'

It was common knowledge that Hugo had no time for Robinson – in common with quite a lot of the staff, but Jonathan was surprised to hear him express it quite so strongly. He felt rather embarrassed by it, and said no more. Nor did Hugo. He rarely indulged in small talk. He saw and did things very large, not cluttering himself.

They came to the folly. 'Only do the traverse if you feel ready for it,' Hugo said. 'You won't find it easy.'

'I'd like to try it.'

The folly, some sixty feet high, was rather like an inland lighthouse, a brick-built, circular tower, tapering slightly towards the top. Over a period of time the brick had weathered and some of the courses were worn enough to give good holds; in other places it had been concreted over purposely to make it more difficult. There were easy routes, marked with paint, with knobs, excrescences and even a crack added, and very difficult places which hardly anybody graduated to. Hugo could climb all over it like an earwig.

'Wales will be a doddle, after this,' he said to Jonathan, smiling.

They both tied on to the rope and Hugo went up the folly to the top, the rope uncoiling steadily after him, Jonathan checking it for snags. The rope was for Hugo, from the top, to safeguard Jonathan; if he had fallen he would have had no safeguard, but Jonathan knew that he no more expected to fall off than a normal person would expect to fall off a good ladder. At the top there was a platform inside, running right round; Jonathan, squinting up, saw Hugo disappear over the top, and then his head reappeared and he called down, 'O.K., you're belayed now. Start when you like.'

Murphy and Partridge appeared just as Jonathan was starting and Murphy said, 'You going to do the traverse then?'

'I hope so,' Jonathan said.

'Gawd. This I must watch.'

They threw themselves down in the shade.

Jonathan knew it was far more fun for them watching him, that watching Hugo; they would also have a considerably longer time in which to relax. He reached up, transferring his weight to the first foothold, and from then on it was a matter of fanatical concentration and willpower – the wall was all but vertical and the holds on this particular pitch ungenerous. He wanted to move smoothly, rhythmically, to look as effortless as Hugo, but in fact he moved painfully, breathlessly, groping and clawing for the meagre finger-holds, grunting with effort. The bricks were warm and he climbed out of the shade of the trees into the full golden heat of the evening sun and felt the sweat running in trickles down over his cheekbones, the hair and the dust sticking and his T-shirt clamming to his back. Down between his ankles, thirty feet below, Murphy and Partridge were spread-eagled, as if pegged out for the ants. He clung, panting, his muscles beginning to ache unmercifully. There was the same to go again, and the hardest bit still above. He remembered the books, and knew that it was done, much harder than this, in frostbite temperatures and icy winds with drops of thousands of feet below the trembling toes, and the way ahead virgin and unknown; Hugo had done it; Hugo had seen his companion die in such conditions, carried away by a stonefall.

'You're doing nicely,' Hugo's voice from above was relaxed and encouraging. 'Make for the corner of the window after the next right foothold. That's where the traverse really starts. The handhold is just above that pale brick.'

He made it sound exceedingly normal, just like a mathematics lesson.

'And so it is,' Jonathan thought, and carried on, feeling like a shoot of ivy slowly growing across the face of the folly. Surely he must be taking hours? Two of his finger-tips were bleeding. Murphy and Partridge got smaller and smaller and the sun got hotter. He was so near it now, like Icarus. He was out of the tops of the trees and could see the Meddington chimneys across a sea of green leaves, afloat, the masts of a steamer hulldown. He felt fantastic.

'Straight across from where you are now, to the lintel of the far window,' Hugo's voice floated down. 'The holds are rather far apart. Try not to rely on fingers too much.'

Right at the end, when it was really bad, he thought he wasn't going to make it. Just for a moment. His knees wouldn't stop trembling and the toehold was infinitesimal, his foot squirming for it inside the sweaty plimsoll and the other foot so far away he thought he would split up the middle. The bricks burned against his cheek, scraping the helmet.

'Oh, God . . .' Spread-eagled, exhausted, he prayed for deliverance. Hugo's voice, close and calm: 'Move your left hand a little to the right, that's easier. Now sort your feet out – the right up to – there's a bit of a bump there. Get that and you've cracked it.'

God speaking. O.K., God, here I come. His hand caught the very top of the brick wall, one of the crenellations, and he grasped it as Stanley had grasped Livingstone.

'Your feet, use your feet,' Hugo said. 'Don't spoil it now – a dignified landfall –' But he was smiling, looking as pleased as if he'd done it himself, and Jonathan landed on the platform beside him, if not dignified, at least with enough self-control to slither into a sitting heap, rather than fall like a stone, which is how he would have preferred. The neat coils of the rope Hugo had taken in supported him. He was knackered.

'Do it every night this week and you'll land up here as if just in from an evening stroll,' Hugo said.

'You think – ?' Jonathan didn't.

'The first time you've got the psychological thing against you – not knowing if you can do it. Now you've solved that one – you'd be surprised. Next time you'll find it a whole lot easier.'

Jonathan grinned and pulled off his helmet. He felt as if he had climbed Everest. His hair was glued to his head. He pushed his fingers into the wet tangled mass but they hurt too much, numb and skinned, and he sucked them instead. His knees were shaking. He pressed them together, to stop them. His mouth was all gritty with brick-dust. Hugo started to drop the rope down to Murphy who was waiting for it.

'Lucky you're not a pianist,' he said, looking at Jonathan's hands. 'You should use your feet more. Remember next time.'

'Is Murphy going to do the traverse?'

'No. He's not up to it yet.'

Good, Jonathan thought fiercely. He felt gloriously happy, sitting up there above the undulating tree-tops getting back his strength, watching Hugo making his belay on Murphy. There was no skin off Hugo's fingers, nor sweat in his tidy hair. He was very brown, very wiry, hard as iron.

'I'm ready when you are,' he shouted down.

Jonathan got to his feet, ready to go.

'Can I do it again tomorrow then?'

'If I'm free, yes. Ask me at lunchtime.'

'O.K., thanks.'

He would like to have stayed, talking, but he had no good reason to, so he climbed down by the staircase inside the tower, exchanged a few sarcasms with the two below and set off down the track back to school. The feeling of deep content and achievement did not leave him. The school was bathed in a sunset glow and breathed nobility from its towers and battlements and for once Jonathan appreciated its offerings. He felt slightly ashamed, in fact, of his normal scorn, and uncomfortable, perversely, that the old heap could give him such pleasure in its curriculum; however, this remorse did not detract from his spirits. He collected some clean clothes, padded along to the bathroom and lowered his sweaty body into a deep, old-fashioned bath, having the whole place to himself. Baths were for prefects only; showers for the masses . . . worth being a prefect for. It was gorgeous, lying there and thinking back on his lovely evening, enveloped in hot, soapy

36

scum, the mind wandering like a horse at grass, picking at pleasant, juicy bits. There was something at the back of it, needling, curious . . . something Hugo had said. A blessed release, he had said, about Robinson's death. For Patsy.

Jonathan washed the parts he could reach without effort, without sitting up, and remembered how, once, he had gone to the houseboat with a message for Robin, and had been discomforted by his glimpse of the domestic situation. he had forgotten it until now but, quite suddenly, it came back vividly, as if it had happened yesterday, cued by Hugo's remark, 'A blessed release.'

It had been quite late, going dark, and he had almost coincided with Patsy's coming home from work. She had been a hundred yards ahead of him. He had arrived at the door just after she had gone inside and had stood there with his hand raised to knock, and heard Robin's voice say petulantly, 'Why are you so late? I'm starving.' The interior of the houseboat had been in darkness, and when Patsy let him in, he had found Robin lying on the sofa.

'What do you want?'

He had explained his mission, a complicated request for some English O-level requirements, urgently needed by Fletcher for some dossier he was compiling, and Robinson had said, 'Oh, you'll have to wait until Patsy's lit the lamps. I can't find a thing in here.'

'Didn't you ring up the electricity people about the generator?' Patsy asked him.

'No. You've got a phone where you work, haven't you? I left it to you.'

'Like every other damned thing,' Patsy said curtly. 'I told you Sister was off this week. I haven't even had time to turn round.'

'I've had a day like that too,' Robin said pathetically, not moving his head off the cushion.

Jonathan could remember his surprise, having seen

with his own eyes Robinson playing billiards in the lunch-hour with Morris out of the biology lab. and, later, sitting out on the patio with a cup of coffee during a free period.

Patsy fetched the paraffin and filled a pressure lamp, cleaned up the spillage and lit it with meths. When the flame flared up he saw her face tight with strain and weariness, a look in her eyes he had never expected her capable of, yet she said to him, kindly, 'Sit down, Meredith. We won't be long. Have a bun.'

She handed him a bag of iced buns and he took one. Robinson never remembered his name as a rule, let alone offered iced buns. Everyone liked Patsy.

She lit the oven and put a pie in to hot up, and put some potatoes in a bowl to peel. Then she took the lamp and started hunting around amongst some shelves of papers, and found him the list Fletcher had asked for. He thanked her and she came to the door and saw him out. When he was half-way across the gangplank he could hear Robinson shouting at her in the same way as he shouted at a class out of control. It had been a shock, something one did not equate with a great poet.

He lay back in the bath, his feet up on the taps, considering Parsons's plastic duck which was nesting in the soap dish, and saw that Hugo might well have been right. There was another incident too, when he came to think of it, which had always rankled, an example of flagrant injustice. Funny how things came back to you, touched off by a chance remark. He remembered this incident with a genuine surge of anger even now, two years later. It had been direct confrontation, his word against Robinson's, and Robinson had won, because he was authority. Fletcher, to give him his due, had been worried, even conspiratorial.

'He said you did it, Meredith. He said there were only three of you there, and you were the only one capable, the only one who can draw.'

'It was on the board when we went in. We were just standing there looking at it. Laughing, I suppose.'

'He said you still had the chalk in your hand.'

'I didn't have any chalk in my hand.'

The awful feeling came back, even now, the helpless feeling of defending oneself against greater powers, having no proof, not having his word trusted. The somewhat obscene and very funny drawing of – unmistakably – Robin conducting a class, all of them out of control, had been examined by both Fletcher and the art master, and they had both been dubious, but diffident in the face of Robin's almost hysterical rage.

'Of course he denies it! – he's not George Washington! He's just a typical, spoilt, public-school moron, smearing what he hasn't the sensibility to understand. They're all the same, in the face of anything that requires fine feelings – for all we do for them – they're coarse, they're cheap – they drag you down –'

'Steady on, Robinson old man,' Fletcher said anxiously. 'It's not that serious, you know. A sense of humour and all that –'

'A sense of humour! Where's humour in that? Mockery, yes, mockery and sneering and derision and scorn towards a mind they will never understand nor appreciate, that they are too crude to ever begin to take nourishment from –' All good, poetical stuff, Jonathan thought, amazed at the conceit, the prejudice, the lack of pure sense being displayed, slightly dismayed, should the truth be known, that such sentiments were in charge of his education.

'Did you do it, Meredith?' Fletcher asked sharply, cutting in, perhaps feeling the same about the scene.

'No, sir.'

'Isn't that good enough for you, Robinson? This boy is not a liar, I can vouch for it.'

'No, I won't accept it. I saw him laughing, sniggering over it, the chalk in his hand. I insist that he is punished for it. He can do a detention this afternoon. I will sit in with him myself.'

'Not this afternoon, Robinson. It's the gala.'

'Splendid. He will miss it.'

Jonathan was outraged. Fletcher, seeing his face, put a hand sharply on his shoulder and said, 'Don't say anything you might regret, Meredith. There are some things in this life you have to accept, whether you like it or not. Good training for later on.' He was given to pontificating, but Jonathan knew that he was on his side, the only crumb of comfort in the whole sordid business.

It was only later in the day, while he was actually doing the detention, alone in the room under the supervision of Robin himself, listening to the distant sounds of pure enjoyment coming from the playing fields and the swimming-pool, that he began to suspect that there was possibly an ulterior motive in Robin's behaviour. The climax of the gala, the part that everyone most looked forward to and that he was so galled to be missing, came at the end of the swimming races when the staff, fully-dressed, all got thrown into the pool by the upper school. It was the high spot of the school year, hugely enjoyed by everybody, even the staff, who dressed for the occasion in a motley assortment of costumes and took part in the spirit expected. Listening to the distant hullabaloo from his forlorn task, bitterly angry at his treatment and at missing the fun, he looked up and saw Robin watching him with a very strange expression on his face. It was one of supreme complacency and content – of having won, Jonathan thought. And at the same moment it occurred to him that Robin had engineered it to avoid being thrown in the pool. Not in so far as he had faked the drawing, but he had used it to his advantage, dumped a detention on the first person who came to hand in order to parade a martyred devotion to duty, instead of losing his dignity, floundering about in the shallow end of the school pool and revealing to all his total inadequacy as any sort of a sports-

40

man. He had hated it the first time it had happened to him; Jonathan could remember his barely-concealed anger, his long blond curls flattened thinly over his skull, eyes glittering sourly at his predicament. Nobody else had ever taken it with such ill-humour, even those far less suited by frame and figure to a dunking. It all made sense then. Jonathan had put down his pen and sat back and watched him in genuine, analytical fascination, that a man so self-professedly superior could sink to such depths in order not to be made fun of.

From that time on, Jonathan had never any use for Robinson. He realized that he had not been surprised by Hugo's remark at all, only that he had made it out loud. A happy release for the whole school, as well as Patsy. Who was upset?

Only Ashworth.

He was back in his room, sprawling on his bed listening to his transistor, when Ashworth came in.

'Oh, jeez, I've been looking for you all over,' Ashworth said. 'Where've you been?'

'Out.'

'Oh, Meredith, I'm in a bloody awful fix. I told you – about Robinson, I mean. He really did commit suicide – there's a letter and everything saying so, in his writing, and that police inspector said – oh, God, I feel terrible about it – I feel awful –'

He sat on his bed, flabby and pathetic, and big baby tears welled up over his pale eyeballs. Jonathan looked at him with great distaste, but a native mercy softened his voice.

'Look, daftie, he wouldn't do such a terrible thing just because of what you did in a lesson. There must be a whole lot more to it than that. You're getting it out of proportion.'

'It could have been – you – know – the last straw. The Inspector said that.'

'Yes, but even then you're not to blame for *his* state of mind, are you? If we were all so much influenced by

41

other people – it's not logical, Ashworth. Calm your-self, boy. In a day or two, when the shock's worn off, you'll see it more clearly.'

'I've got to go to the inquest.'

'Oh.'

'Just in case – I won't have to say anything, probably, he said, but I might –' large hiccup of self-pity. 'Meredith, if I have to go, will you come with me? I shall die.'

'It's nothing to do with me, is it? I'm not invited. I can't just amble along, to hold your hand. Don't be so feeble, Ashworth. Go to bed and go to sleep. You'll see it all much better in the morning.'

Irritably Jonathan pulled his own clothes off and reached for his pyjamas, anxious to stop Ashworth's drip of misery on his own content. He didn't for a mo-ment think Ashworth need have anything to worry about, for countless boys had behaved in the same way without someone committing suicide on them, but Ashworth wasn't going to see it that way – at least, not tonight. Ashworth slowly followed his example, heav-ing himself into bed with his usual threshings and grunt-ings like an old dog making itself comfortable in its basket. Jonathan pulled the light cord, and lay looking at the square of night out of the window, the deep elec-tric blue of the summer dusk. He felt soothed again, and the happiness came back, at what he had done, and Wales to come . . . it was almost too good to be true.

He was on the edge of sleep, drifting, when Ashworth said, as an afterthought, sounding sleepy himself, 'You know you said you saw Hugo down there last night? On Robinson's boat.'

'Mmm.'

'Well, did you? Truly?'

'Why?'

'Well, I was stuck with that Inspector all morning, and at one stage Hugo came in for something, and the Inspector asked him the routine questions – when did he

42

last see Robinson – and Hugo said in the staff-room at four o'clock. The Inspector said, "I understand your house is down towards the river, not far from the boat. You didn't see him later, after school?" and Hugo said no.'

Jonathan said nothing. He felt his body contract in a curious, frightened way, shocked.

'But you said you saw him,' Ashworth said.

'I must have been mistaken,' Jonathan said tightly.

But he knew he wasn't.

CHAPTER
2

Jonathan slept badly and woke early, feeling miserable. After a few moments, he remembered why. He lay looking at the ceiling, not sure why it mattered. Hugo lying . . . he must have his reasons, but it seemed to Jonathan an extraordinarily out-of-character impulse. He could not see that there was any reason for it unless Hugo, like Ashworth, had a conscience about what Robinson had done. The mind boggled. Whichever way one looked at it, it was all wrong. Jonathan had never supposed Hugo capable of doing anything wrong: hence feeling miserable.

He turned over angrily, realized that it was going to be another sweating hot day and decided to go down to the swimming pool. He liked swimming on his own, and before breakfast was about the only chance. At the moment, as things were, he would only swim on his own, being unduly sensitive about the scars on his back, which, so far, it was only Ashworth's privilege to see. Ashworth, reversing the roles, told Jonathan he was an idiot to bother, but Jonathan supposed his prickliness was really due to his conviction that he was indeed an idiot – to have got potted at by a lunatic with a gun through a complete misunderstanding which he should have had the wit to foresee. Ashworth, by the habitual abysmal confusion of his thought processes, seemed to think there was something heroic about getting shot in the back, but Jonathan was ashamed of it.

The pool, still and blue beneath the rampant vegetation, looked as if it could well sport crocodiles; one was prompted to peer nervously behind the roots and shrubs round the periphery. But all was still and cool; the sun had not yet struck the roof, being impeded by an added science wing; there was a heady scent of mimosa mixed with chlorine, and the water was warm, almost too warm. Jonathan, surfacing from his initial dive, had the same feeling as he had the evening before: was he fair, knocking Meddington, when he so much enjoyed quite a reasonable proportion of what it offered? This exotic pool with its jungle trappings was far removed from the normal school provision. Even the floor of the bath was tiled in Romanesque patterns which undulated as one swam down, like patterns in a kaleidoscope; the tiled flowers waved on their stems like the water-lilies in one of the scooped backwaters of the river. Jonathan felt he could pick them. He put a hand down and touched bottom, turned over and through the clear water saw the real leaves of the passion-flower arched high above against the pale early morning sky. It was quite beautiful, the tracery of Paxton's glass roof spidered over the dawn where the creeper had left gaps, and the sun swimming through the water over his eyeballs, more like being in some Aegean grotto than a public bath. Very nice, thought Jonathan, and saw a face there, wrinkled by the movement on the water, startling him out of his dreams.

'Hullo,' Hugo said, as he surfaced. 'I thought I was the only person awake.'

He swam, very early, to keep fit, but Jonathan had never been so early before. He didn't know what to say, not having slept because of Hugo. He trod water, trying to think of something non-committal.

But Hugo said, 'I thought you didn't swim any more. You don't come to life-saving classes.'

'No.'

'Because of your back?'

'Yes.'

'Not very sensible. Could you save someone if they went in the river? If you'd seen Robinson, for example?'

Jonathan, still thinking that Hugo was hiding something about Robinson's death, was floored by this question. He shook his head.

'I – I don't know.'

'You might be very sorry, one day, if you don't learn while you've got the opportunity.'

Jonathan swam to the side and pulled himself out. He still found it hard to believe that Hugo had told that lie. He wanted to ask him, but couldn't. He knew he hadn't been mistaken. He stood in front of him, silent, prodding with his bare toe at the patterns in the mosaic: flowers again, the drops of water from his body beading their geometrical petals. He felt he had been far away under the water, and couldn't cope now, suddenly.

But Hugo smiled and said, 'For heaven's sake, I've seen worse scars from acne. I'll expect you back in the senior class on Friday.'

It seemed quite prosaic then, nothing out of place at all. Jonathan reached for his towel and wrapped it round him.

'All right.' He would decide later. He still didn't want to go but wasn't going to say so. He nodded towards the water. 'It's all yours. I've got some homework to do before breakfast.'

He went back to his room and got dried. Ashworth, in his usual dull, uninquisitive fashion, had forgotten all about the remark he had thrown into the gloaming the night before, which had given Jonathan insomnia, but Jonathan did not want to pursue it, and was glad. It was something he wanted to drop out of his mind.

In the evening Ashworth was summoned to the Head

Master's office and informed that he was to attend the inquest on the defunct Robinson, in the remote possibility that he might be required to give evidence.

'They say there is so little evidence concerning his state of mind. Apparently he hadn't had a row with his wife, he wasn't being blackmailed, he hadn't had any bad news, and the only actual thing that had made him unhappy that day was us. Me particularly.' Ashworth, reporting back, white and wretched, sat on his bed and gazed at Jonathan in despair.

Jonathan, imagining himself in the same position, said gently, 'But it's still not your fault. Thousands of schoolteachers every year would commit suicide if that's all there is to it.'

'It doesn't seem to have been anyone else's fault, all the same. By the way, Meredith, I know you'll be mad, but I asked if you could come with me to the inquest and Armstrong said yes. I said I'd feel scared stiff and he said I could bring a friend and we could have lunch out afterwards, and the rest of the day off.'

A day spent in Ashworth's company, inquest or no inquest, was Jonathan's idea of a fate worse than death, but he was too kind to demur. He merely made a face, and asked, 'When is it?'

'Friday.'

By the time Friday came Jonathan had recovered from his doubts about Hugo's infallibility, having completed two more highly satisfying climbs on the folly and spent half an hour each time recovering in the evening sunshine on the top platform discussing techniques while Murphy on the rope below failed to do once what he had now done three times.

'You're a natural,' Hugo told him. 'Natural balance and the right temperament. When we go to Wales I'll take you on a real climb. A hard one. Show you what it's all about.' The expedition to Wales dominated Jonathan's thinking. He had never looked forward to anything as much.

Friday came as a distinct impediment to his content. Ashworth was in a deeply gloomy state which made his company about as lively as a suet pudding. They dressed in their best ties and blazers, although it was another scorcher, and presented themselves at the Head's office at nine-thirty as instructed. Mr Armstrong was there with Patsy Robinson. Only the four of them were going.

Although Patsy was perfectly composed and the Head even jocular, the essential seriousness of the expedition was marked. Jonathan felt a great and unexpected sadness fall on him like a shroud, passing into the sunless study, saying good-morning to Patsy, and then waiting in silence while Armstrong briefed his secretary for the day. Up till now he had avoided thinking about what had actually happened, but now it struck him as a quite awful thing to die in the middle of such a fantastic summer, at the age of twenty-seven. Instinct more than logic prompted his thinking. Robinson apparently had chosen it. Jonathan found it hard to believe.

Patsy was saying to Ashworth, 'Don't look so worried! It's highly unlikely you'll have to say anything.'

She would, Jonathan presumed. Everyone liked Patsy, just as everyone had disliked Robin. She was small and quick and busy, but with an apparently tranquil mind, and a slow, sweet smile. Unlike most active people, she did not say much. She gave the impression of being a strong character, which is why everyone thought it odd she should have 'wasted herself' – the term most often used – on Robin, who had given quite the opposite effect. She was a nurse and worked in the hospital at Thorntonhill, often on nights. She had been at work the night Robinson drowned.

The Head having finished his business, they went out to his car and drove off towards Thorntonhill. The road followed the river most of the way and Jonathan watched it out of the window, the part Robinson must have drowned in, a very fast and beautiful river much prized for trout, the water deep and clear and rapid. He remembered that it was Friday and he would miss his life-saving lesson whether he wanted to or not, and he remembered the strange remark of Hugo's, about could he have rescued Robinson? Well, who knew what one could do in the heat of the moment? – but Jonathan thought, on the whole, no. Not if he had struggled. The river was notoriously dangerous. He wasn't sorry when the road left the lush cow pastures and beds of yellow flags and veered into the outskirts of Thorntonhill. Armstrong threaded his way through the congested traffic of the small market-town and managed to find a parking place close to the court-room.

He glanced at his watch. 'Just in nice time.'

The court-room was gloomy and austere, but it was filled with people apparently perfectly happy in their work: newspaper reporters and policemen chatting, ushers telling them where to sit, clerks laying out papers on various tables and arranging the bits and pieces on the coroner's desk. Just everyday stuff to them, Jonathan realized, if not to poor Patsy, and Ashworth who had gone zombie with fright. Jonathan steered him and sat him down and fed him a few peppermints while they waited. Patsy sat on his other side and he could see her fingers tightly clasped in her lap and sensed that she was as frightened as Ashworth. He didn't see why. Tense and miserable, yes, but not, for her, frightened. He looked at her. She had beads of sweat on her upper lip. It made him feel uneasy too. He ate one of his own peppermints and offered one to her and Mr Armstrong said to him, quite sharply, 'No *eating*, Meredith.'

'Oh, jeez,' thought Jonathan, in despair. What a way to spend a day! It wasn't anything to do with him at all.

Someone thumped for silence and they all stood up as the coroner came in. Bad luck for him too, Jonathan thought; he was probably retired and would rather be taking elevenses on the lawn with his wife and *The Times*, preparatory to tidying the dead roses. He looked that sort. Instead of tidying the dead bodies.

But it wasn't at all complicated.

A policeman described being called to the weir by a fisherman early in the morning to deal with a body that had come down on the current and got caught across the sluice gate. The body was recovered, identified as that of Lindsay Robinson, resident at Meddington, and examined to establish the cause of death which was asphyxia by drowning.

The Detective-Inspector who had visited the school then took the witness-box and recounted the facts he had uncovered. He described finding a note on the table in the saloon of the houseboat, a message in Robinson's handwriting saying, 'I think this is the best way to end it.' He said that there seemed to be no evidence suggesting that Robinson had any good reason for taking his own life, apart from the fact that he seemed to have had a more than usually tiresome day's teaching.

'He was stated by several witnesses to be extremely upset at the end of the last lesson of the afternoon, owing to some trick his class played on him. It was apparently not uncommon for him to lose control of his class. Mr Armstrong, the Head Master, will acknowledge this.' The Inspector glanced at Armstrong, who looked grieved at the allegation but was obviously not going to deny it, and back to his notes. 'Nobody appears to have seen or spoken to the deceased after he left the staff-room at approximately five o'clock and went back to the houseboat which is his home. His wife had already left to go to work. She is a staff-nurse at the General Hospital and was on night-duty. She had left his supper in the oven. He ate it and left the dishes in the sink. There was a pile of exercise books on the table, which he had marked, and the note was lying beside them. There were no signs of violence, or anything out of place, neither below nor on deck.'

Jonathan, listening to the recital, was acutely aware of what he had seen that night, and tried to forget. It hadn't occurred to him that, coming to the inquest

50

merely to steady Ashworth's nerves, his own raw memory was going to be jogged again. He had carefully put his knowledge out of his head, so successfully in fact, that it came now with a sense of fresh shock. It occurred to him that he harboured a valuable piece of evidence; he should be in the witness-box himself, telling them that Robinson had been alive and well, happy even, at ten o'clock that night. He had been sitting in a deckchair, and Jonathan had heard him laugh. Charles Hugo had been sitting on the hatch, but he hadn't been laughing. Jonathan had got the impression that he had been angry – at least, not amused. They hadn't been laughing together, in a social sort of way. The mental picture of the two of them together, in the dusk, the glow of Robin's cigarette end, the whine of a mosquito, was no less sharp now for having been so carefully obliterated from Jonathan's mind since Ashworth's bombshell remark about Hugo saying he hadn't been there. He remembered it with the same overwhelming feeling of despair that he had experienced the first time. He was as moved now, as deep in the wretched affair, as both Ashworth and Patsy.

Patsy was now called to give evidence. She got up, leaving her handbag on her seat, and went to the witness-box.

'Mrs Patricia Helen Robinson, the wife of the deceased?'

Patsy agreed, and said in reply to the coroner's next question that, no, her husband hadn't seemed to her to be distressed in any way the last time she had seen him, although he had always been subject to moods of depression.

'There had been no differences between you, no quarrels?'

'No.'

'When did you last see him?'

'When he left for school in the morning. He was on duty at lunch-time so he didn't come back then, as he sometimes does. I left for work at four in the afternoon, and I didn't see him again.'

'And you got home at eight the following morning?'

'Yes.'

'Had your husband, to your knowledge, been alone on the boat the evening before?'

'As far as I know. There was no sign of anyone else having been there.'

'No sign at all of anything out of the ordinary?'

'No, except the note. It was on the table. The Inspector hadn't moved it. He showed it to me.'

'I have it here. You will confirm that this is the note, and this is your husband's handwriting?'

Patsy was crying. The usher took her the note and she groped for a handkerchief, without success, and said she had left her glasses in her handbag.

Armstrong picked up her handbag from the seat beside him and said to Jonathan, 'Take it to her.'

Jonathan did as he was told, climbing the two steps up to the witness-box. She was holding the note in her hand, and he got a good view of it, Robin's usual sprawl spreading across a sheet of exercise-book paper in red biro, saying, 'I think this is the best way to end it.' Underneath was a strong line going off the left-hand side of the paper.

'Thank you,' Patsy said to him. She took the bag, appeared to pull herself together somewhat, and Jonathan retreated.

'You are perfectly certain that that is your husband's handwriting?' the coroner insisted.

'Yes.'

'It is very brief, one might almost say curt. You found nothing else of a more personal nature?'

'No.'

'You say you really cannot think of any reason why he should have taken his own life?'

'No.'

'You were on good terms with one another?'

Patsy hesitated. Then she said angrily, 'We always quarrelled a lot. But there was no particular trouble when – when this happened. If it wasn't for the note, I would – I wouldn't believe it. He might have *fallen* overboard. That would be easy enough. He doesn't swim very well. But with the note – I –'

The coroner was staring at her. Anyone less strong-willed, Jonathan thought, would have crumpled up under that bifocalized stare. But Patsy visibly pulled herself together, and stared back. The coroner blinked.

'I am sorry to distress you, asking these questions,' he said rather more gently. 'But you understand that this is the reason for this gathering. I don't think I need ask you any more.'

Patsy came back to her seat, silent tears rolling down her cheeks. Jonathan tried to think what it must be like, living with someone, every day the two of you together, and then with no warning – snap. He couldn't imagine it. One's whole way of life, one's routine habit, bound up as it must be in the other person, severed without warning. No wonder she was adrift. He wanted to think of anything but the one thing that disturbed him.

The doctor gave evidence to say that Robinson had died of asphyxia due to drowning, with no other marks or indications on the body to show how he had come to be in the water. He had been in perfect health, although he had been treated in the past for nervous depression. The coroner seemed pleased to hear of this.

'It does seem,' he said, 'that the deceased took his own life, and we can only assume that it was due to some fit of depression brought about by a bad day at work, or possibly because of some disappointment or feeling of failure that we have no way of comprehending. I will therefore bring in a verdict of suicide, and the court will adjourn for lunch.'

There was no dissent or surprise, everyone merely gathering up their papers and getting to their feet. A reporter appeared to ask if he could speak to Mrs

Robinson, and Armstrong said to Jonathan and Ashworth, 'I suggest you two go off and amuse yourselves for the rest of the day. You've got bus fares to get back? Here – get yourselves something to eat.' He gave them a pound each, and enough for the bus. 'You must be back in time for supper, O.K.?'

'Thank you, sir.'

They were both, for their two separate reasons, depressed by the morning's work, and went out into the sunshine without any lifting of the spirits.

'Funny nobody knowing about Hugo being down there that night,' Ashworth said.

'I must have got it wrong,' Jonathan said, knowing that he hadn't.

'Yeah, pity. I've really got something on my conscience, haven't I? The only bloody reason they could find for him doing himself in –'

'Oh, pack it in Ashworth! If anyone had thought you were to blame you'd be in the doghouse now, not given the day off and a whole lousy pound to spend on sweeties.'

'Yeah, well, nobody actually says anything, do they? But they think it. *I* think it. You didn't see him fly off the handle, did you? Just like a maniac, he was, screaming –'

'That's the point – he wasn't normal, was he? Nobody else in the school goes berserk like that just because he's played up a bit, do they? You've never seen Fletcher like it, or Armstrong, or any of them . . . '

They crossed the road and stood on the old stone bridge over the river, leaning on the parapet, scratching at the tiny cushions of lichen, scowling down at the water. It was boiling hot and they took off their blazers, but daren't roll up their sleeves or loosen their ties, knowing Armstrong was at large. 'Might as well go back really,' Ashworth said, and they both went on scowling, flapping at the midges, fed up.

'Let's go and get some ice-cream.'

54

They spent their money quite easily on ice-cream, coke, doughnuts and magazines and then went to the bus-stop.

Ashworth, staring unseeingly at the pavement, said, 'If it wasn't for the note I'd have said Hugo *murdered* him. That's why he never said.'

'God, what a thing to say –'

'It'd be better for me. I wish he had.'

'Jeez, Ashworth, you can't go round saying things like that. I was wrong about seeing him. Forget it, for heaven's sake.'

'Well –'

'Anyway, there's no motive.'

'What d'you mean?'

'There has to be a motive for murder.'

Ashworth thought hard for a minute and said, 'He's in love with Patsy.'

Jonathan laughed.

The bus hove into sight round the corner of the Town Hall, grinding its gears wearily.

'I wish it was true,' Ashworth said. 'It would let me out.'

CHAPTER
3

'The memorial service for Mr Robinson on Sunday morning in the chapel is obligatory for the sixth form.'

Mr Fletcher dropped this unwelcome item of news without expression, and it was politely received in the same vein, no comment. Jonathan felt gloom at the prospect settle in his innards like a lead pudding. The funeral having been private and the school not invited, he thought that the whole nasty subject of Robinson could safely be forgotten, but, no – Robinson must be officially, compulsorily remembered, and all the uneasy things Jonathan knew about the business and had kept hidden would have to be remembered yet again. Ashworth felt the same, perhaps more so. On Sunday morning they changed stonily out of Sunday clothes – frayed jeans and T-shirts – into deadly best uniform and filed into the bilious gloom of the Gothic chapel, where the blazing sunlight, entering through screens of flamboyant Victorian stained glass, cast unlikely complexions upon the congregation. Jonathan, keeping well at the back and hoping to go into a coma for the duration, was somewhat dismayed to find himself joined by Iris Webster. He already had the emotional Ashworth on one side, and was not in the mood to cope. Iris, sitting in an unfortunate shaft of amber light, looked more like a frog than ever, a grey-blue dress like a storm-cloud darkened to toad-khaki, her white face gilded and her eyes glassy-gold with trying to be composed. Jonathan took one look at her and sensed distress signals flying, and sunk lower in his pew. The only way to endure was to remember that on Wednesday they were going to Wales to climb on real rock.

His eyes falling upon the pillar two pews ahead, he decided to spend the service plotting an ascent to the hammer-beam roof by way of this same pillar, a traverse of the clerestory to the rood-screen – lots of holds there – a belay over the flagstaff of the school banner and up the south face of the chancel arch to the keystone and on to the sheer face of the nave which, having been plastered over, was going to be somewhat of a problem. It might be better the other side, the north face of the chancel, but – not being in the choir and being able to see the alternative – he wasn't sure. Possibly the corner where the clerestory met the end wall, with a belay over the memorial (nice and knobbly) to Sir Bracewell Gibbons, Bart., would provide enough holds, the bare stone showing through. It was interesting enough to arouse a faint hope that he might actually be able to attempt it (would Hugo allow it? Answer, no, but he would be sympathetic). Perhaps at night, with Murphy, and a good moon – but dreadful to go splat on the tiled floor. They'd only have to lay a fresh stone over the mess: 'Memorial to Jonathan Meredith, a pupil of this school . . .' And another memorial service, obligatory for Sixth formers, and another good Sunday gone phut. Jonathan sat and thought about falling off for a bit, or getting one's back broken and spending the rest of life in a wheel-chair . . . what did one do? Take up something sedentary but mind-stretching, wood-carving or the violin, no good for the piano because you wouldn't be able to use the pedal . . . at this point they had to stand up to sing a hymn, and as the organ (completely useless for an invalid, as complex as driving a four-in-hand) soared into the arches of the roof, Jonathan saw the tears spilling down Iris's cheeks and positively splashing on the floor. He felt acutely embarrassed, and prayed urgently to God, 'Please don't let her faint. Don't do that to me again.' And then he became aware, with horror, that Ashworth was sniffing too; a great baby tear welled down his furry, pimply cheek, pure self-pity for his guilt complex. Jonathan, surrounded by tears, felt panic rising, and anger, and confusion, and fell on his knees gratefully for the ensuing prayers, hiding from the awful sight with a pretence at reverence. He really was bad when it came to emotions. Not so much Ashworth – the *idiot*! – but poor froggy Iris whom tough Jane despised and nobody seemed to care for, fastening her affections on the wet poet – one could only pity her for her appalling taste and consequent misery.

When the service was over he noticed that Iris went off alone, the other girls ganging up in their usual noisy, arrogant fashion and going off to change into shorts and bikinis. He managed to avoid Ashworth who had got into a conversation about motorbikes and was quite spry once out of the church atmosphere, hared up to his room and changed back into jeans and set off for the folly where he had arranged to meet Murphy and Pettifer and some of the others to get some training in. He took his own path through the woods, a quicker, if more tangled, way than the accepted one, and was bulldozing his passage through an encroachment of wild rose suckers, swearing slightly, when he all but fell over a pair of legs. He was as startled as the owner of the legs, who let out a shriek.

'Jeez, I'm sorry!'

It was Iris, curled in a damp, diaphanous ball under the honeysuckle like an animal gone to ground, so evidently far gone in despair that Jonathan realized she could scarcely be ignored. Without any joy at all he

stopped and surveyed the situation. The only construc-
tive thought that came into his head was that he would
have saved himself a whole lot of trouble if he'd taken
the proper path. God, *Robinson*! he thought furiously –
the man was really wasting his day one way and
another.

'Hey, Iris,' he said, feeling stupid.

She had her head buried in her arms and was not only
shaking with sobs, but was moaning as well. He thought
for a moment that perhaps he ought to go and get Miss
Slater or Mrs Arthurs or somebody, but it would take
ages finding them on a Sunday and he still had hopes of
making it to the folly before lunch. If he could get her
moving he could steer her back to help and sympathy.
From whom? his mind added, and his heart sank for
her.

'Hey, look, it's not that bad,' he said hopefully, and
squatted down beside her. 'You can't carry on like
this.'

He put a hand on her shoulder, hoping to unroll her.
It was a First Aid thing really. He ought to be in a black
uniform with an armband. The woods were very dense
and silent and – but for him – she had chosen her
solitude well. One could die here quite well, if no one
was looking. Perhaps that was what she wanted?

'Listen, it'll be all right in a bit. Do shut up. You'll
make yourself ill.'

'I want to die,' she said, muffled and streaming.

Oh well, he had been right on that point. He sat down
in the warm, leafy humus, not sure what to say next.
Perhaps there was no great hurry. There were no signs
of life in the wood, apart from animal, and silence from
the direction of the folly. Perhaps Murphy and co. had
meant after lunch? He couldn't climb on his own. It was
forbidden.

'Shall I fetch Jane or somebody?' he asked.

'No. I hate them. I hate them all.'

No comment. They were pretty awful, after all.

'Well, it's end of term next week. It'll be all right when you get home, won't it? You can forget it all then.'

'No. It's worse at home.'

'What, worse than here?'

'Yes, far worse.'

God Almighty, he thought! The mind boggled.

Genuinely curious, he said, 'It can't be worse than now, surely?'

'Oh, it can,' she said stubbornly.

She lifted her head for a moment out of her arms, and looked at him through her sea of tears.

'Oh, it's you,' she said, revealing a faint interest, enough to unroll slightly and go on watching him.

'You don't go round like this at home all the time?' Jonathan was trying to picture it, and couldn't imagine it at all.

'I'm not any happier, if that's what you mean. I perhaps don't cry all the time though. I only cry when I'm on my own.'

'Oh.' Jeez, he thought, what a prospect! Sometimes he had thought he wasn't all that happy at home, not entirely, but he still mostly had a jolly good time when he was there.

'Why, what happens? Do they beat you up?'

She didn't answer, and Jonathan wished he hadn't asked. It might have been interpreted as frivolous. But she did wriggle up on to one elbow, and sniff as if she meant to stop crying, although the tears kept on rolling.

She said, 'You don't have to bother with me, you know.'

He shrugged. 'I'm not going anywhere,' he said, having decided that the others had meant after lunch. Anyway he was curious now about the wretched girl's home life.

'You mean you're not miserable just because of – of Mr Robinson? There's more to it than that?'

'No, it's Mr Robinson,' she said, with a fresh upsurging of tears. And then, 'But there's nothing else to make me feel happy either.'

'But loving Mr Robinson wasn't going to make you happy, was it? He didn't love you, did he?'

'No, of course not. But I could watch him. That made me happy. Now there's nothing.'

Perhaps a bit in the same way as he liked Hugo being there, someone as a sort of cornerstone. If she called it being in love, that was her business. He didn't. But he felt for her, all the same. She was a very *peculiar* girl. It didn't make for happiness, being so peculiar, and not having any friends. She groped for a handkerchief and started to mop up.

'I'm sorry,' she said.

He felt embarrassed.

'Well –'

'You needn't have stopped. I didn't mean anyone to find me. I didn't think anyone came here. I didn't want anyone.'

'No. I'm sorry.'

'No, not you. The girls, I mean.'

'Don't you like any of them?'

'No. But it's my fault, I suppose.'

'I don't think so. They're awful.'

'I thought it couldn't be worse here than home.'

'And it is?'

'It's as bad. I can't bear the thought of going home, and it's dreadful here.'

She sobbed with complete abandon then, laying her head into her arms again, her whole body heaving. Jonathan sat back against a tree, silent, watching her. Whatever was there to say to that? He picked a honeysuckle flower and sucked at its sweetness, waiting. A cuckoo was calling somewhere. He could picture the roast beef in the ovens back at school and smell it in his mind: they always ate well on Sundays. She might feel better after a square meal. She was frightfully thin. He was ravenous.

After a bit he said, 'Isn't there anybody?' He couldn't imagine there not being anybody. 'Your parents can't be that awful?' But some must be, by the nature of things.

After another bout of mopping and sniffing, she said, 'My mother doesn't want me because I get in the way of her concerts and practising – she's called Anastasia O'Neal – have you heard of her? She's a cellist.'

'Yes.'

'She's got a flat in the Bayswater Road. I can't have anybody in and she's glad when I'm out. She makes me practise all the time I'm home. Or we go to New York or Berlin or somewhere and I have to stay in the hotel and go out to dinner with awful boring people. She won't let me wander about. She always finds me somewhere to practise, and awful foreign teachers who can't talk English. She thinks that's all there is – practising. I hate her. I just hate it all.'

'Oh.' Not so good by the sound of it.

'My father left years ago. He never comes any more.'

Not surprising, Jonathan thought.

'What do you do?' she asked him. She lifted her head and her brimming eyes fixed him abruptly. 'What will you do when you go home?'

Jeez, he thought, whatever to say to appease her? He didn't do anything exactly.

'What do you do?' she insisted.

He tried to think. 'I lie around, potter about. Play records. Ride my horse a bit, go in for a few competitions. Go around with my friends, – unless that idiot, McNair, had got himself a job since I last saw him – 'Go on holiday if anything's fixed. I think my ma said something about Ireland at the end of August – she's got an aunt there. It's quite nice.'

'Have you got any brothers or sisters?'

'I've got a sister, Jessica. Younger than me.'

'What are your parents like?'

Hard to say. Easy to *think*, sometimes. Sometimes he hated his mother, but it generally passed off after a bit.

She was very intelligent and tactful, and she noticed, and it got smoothed over somehow. Leaving him a bit confused. But he didn't hate her as Iris seemed to hate hers. He knew, deep down and not to be admitted, that if he didn't get on with his mother quite a lot of the fault was his.

'My father's O.K.,' he said. 'Not there very often though.'

'And your mother?'

He considered how to put it. 'She's O.K. if you do what she wants.'

'Do you?'

'Well, quite a lot of the time, yes. It's not that she wants anything too awful. But I want to be left alone mostly.'

'Is she sympathetic?'

'No. I wouldn't call her that.' But he didn't particularly want sympathy, did he? Not like Iris wanted it. Iris was pathetic, having nothing, and nobody.

'I'm dreading the end of term,' she said. 'I'd rather die first.'

Jonathan felt worried. Having been lulled into playing father confessor, he didn't want any responsibilities on his hands. 'It's no good thinking like that,' he said.

'No, but you can't alter what's true.'

'I think you should come back to school. Perhaps you could talk to somebody about it, who could help.'

'Who?'

Jonathan scowled. She had a way of touching the nitty-gritty that was unnerving. There wasn't anybody, of course.

'Talking to you is better than anybody I've come across so far in Meddington. But you're not here because you want to be, only because you tripped over me. You could have walked on, of course.'

Jonathan sensed danger lights flashing. He stood up. 'You *are* all right?' Who was he trying to convince?

'I'm as all right as possible under the circumstances.'

She wasn't even trying to be funny, merely honest. 'Well, come back then. I'm going back now. It's lunchtime.'

It was a fantastically noble offer, to escort her back publicly across the lawns to Meddington, in front of all the ghastly sunbathing females and snide friends who would make appalling remarks to him afterwards, and he was fantastically relieved that she turned it down.

'No. I promise you I'm all right – enough, I mean – not to worry. Don't tell anybody, will you? I just want to be on my own. Today. Tomorrow will be better. Don't send anybody.'

'Not if you don't want.'

She was a whole lot better now than when he first tripped over her.

'You are very kind,' she said.

He felt extremely embarrassed, and walked away, churned up with worry about what he might have set in motion. He didn't want her to get any wrong ideas. She wasn't the sort of girl he went for although, as a person, she was all right. She wasn't as affected as she looked. And it was only a matter of opinion as to whether her draperies were any worse than Jane and co's denims. If she had been a happy and smiling person inside them, who knows . . . ? She might have looked beautiful.

Her utter misery worried him, but he forgot it during an afternoon's climbing and by evening he had something to worry about that put all other contenders out of the running.

'Ashworth's looking for you,' someone said to him at supper.

'He's raving,' somebody else said. 'Out of his mind. Frothing looney.'

'How so?' Jonathan asked nervously.

'Wait till you see him. He will divulge only to you. To Meredith. To no other. Prepare yourself.'

'Divulge what?'

'How should we know? It's for your pure ears alone. The gibberings of Ashworth D.'

Jonathan was not cheered. He had had enough of confidences for one day. He was getting to be the back page of a women's magazine. No one paid him for it.

He went to his room reluctantly and found it empty, much to his relief. He sat on the bed and thought about Iris for a bit. Six days to breaking up, and then what was she going to do? Rather die, she said. But there was really nothing he could do about it. Was there? No. He started to get out his economics prep., not enthusiastic. It was only three days to Wales, and impossible to feel low, even when faced with economics and the incipient Ashworth.

'Jeez, I've been looking for you everywhere, Meredith!' he said, bursting in.

'So I've heard.'

'I've discovered something – oh, cripes, I'm sure I haven't got it wrong, but it's incredible! I've been looking and looking at it, telling myself it can't be true. But only you can possibly decide. Really, Meredith, you won't believe it –'

He was ferreting through his homework books on the table, which Jonathan had pushed to one side. Jonathan watched him with a detached curiosity, unaware of impending doom. Slightly amused, in fact, by Ashworth's elephantine excitement. Oh, happy moment! he remembered, a long time afterwards.

'Look.' Ashworth pulled out an exercise-book, open at the last page of writing. 'This is it. Recognize the writing?'

He pointed to the corrections and comments in red biro down the margin and at the end of the essay.

'Robinson's?' Jonathan humoured him.

'Yes. We got these books back on Friday and I never opened mine until this afternoon. Mrs Robinson brought them back. They're the ones he was correcting the night he snuffed it.'

'And so what?'

'Well, look, I'll explain first what the homework was about. You see he's made a remark at the bottom of the page –'

Ashworth pointed it out with his finger as if Jonathan were aged four. Jonathan read it patiently: 'A good effort but it goes on too long. Finish it while it's still pithy – bang!'

The next page was torn out.

'We had to write an argument between two people, you see. He gave us the opening sentences. Now look – for Christ's sake, Meredith, you must see! He says it's too long. He's drawn a line across the page where he thinks it would be better to end it –' Ashworth's fingers were trembling. The line was about a third of the way down the page. Jonathan read what Ashworth had written and agreed that the piece ended better at Robinson's red line than at the bottom of the page. But no one had ever disputed that Robinson was a good judge of the written word.

'Don't be so bloody thick!' Ashworth said impatiently. 'Don't you see? The page torn out – it had written on it: 'I think this is the best way to end it', and a line drawn across underneath, going off the page. It was supposed to be a suicide note, but it wasn't. It was just his corrections to my English homework!'

Jonathan found this hard to accept, and read the essay from the beginning, knowing that he was prevaricating. He didn't want to accept it. The implications were frightful. He carefully did not think about them. But Ashworth's supposition was unanswerable. He saw the suicide note quite plainly in his mind, as he had seen it at the inquest, and it was most certainly the missing page from Ashworth's exercise book. He wouldn't say it.

'I'm right, aren't I? You must admit it,' Ashworth said belligerently.

'Perhaps.'

'*Perhaps!*' Ashworth repeated with infinite scorn. 'I know why you won't say it. You know what it means? That he never wrote a suicide note at all. And the verdict of suicide was brought in purely because of the note. There was no other reason, no other evidence at all. And who was down there that night? Who lied, and said he wasn't?'

Jonathan wouldn't say it.

'He saw the book lying open and a ready-made suicide note –'

'You are *crazy*, Ashworth!' Jonathan cracked out furiously. 'No one ever said it was *murder*! You can't go round saying things like that –'

'I can – I want it to be, don't you see! Better than it's being *my* fault. How do you think it feels for me? Like in church this morning – everyone knows what happened – they all think it's my fault. I'd far rather he'd been murdered.'

'But look, be sensible. It can't be murder, however much you want it to be. There's just no reason for it. They aren't the sort of people, for heaven's sake!'

'No? You say that just because it's Hugo. You've got this thing about him, like a girl –'

Jonathan swung round and clouted Ashworth across the face with enormous force. Ashworth let out a bellow like a charging bull and fell backwards across the table, crashing it across the room, books and table-lamp flying. As he fell he lashed out with his foot and caught Jonathan painfully on the knee. Jonathan, ordinarily, was not a believer in physical violence, but he was now as fraught as Ashworth, and Ashworth was coming back, blood pouring from his nose, stammering incoherent abuse. Jonathan had no choice but to fend him off, which led to further noisy overturning of chairs, crashing of wardrobe doors and much thumping and grunting and invective as they grappled furiously in the small amount of space. Jonathan hit his head on the corner of his divan, nearly braining himself, and Ashworth got him by the hair and dragged him up for another bash. Jonathan brought his knee up – no one could say they were fighting fair – and Ashworth let out another of his elephantine bellows. At the same moment Jonathan was aware of infiltration: the room was suddenly quite full of people, including Fletcher and Parsons the head prefect and quite a few bystanders in the doorway.

By the time they were disentangled Jonathan had remembered what it was all about. Fletcher asked him the same question. Jonathan said to Ashworth, violently, 'Don't *say* anything –'

'Meredith! You're a *prefect*, for God's sake! We expect sanity – it's a minimum requirement. Do you want to explain?'

'No, sir,' Jonathan said.

'Get this room straight then, the two of you, and then you go with Parsons. Take your blankets and sleep on his floor tonight. Ashworth, you stay here, at your peril. We'll talk about it in class in the morning. You can work on it, Parsons, meanwhile. It's really not sixth form behaviour.'

He supervised the tidying up, and Jonathan managed to say to Ashworth, 'Keep it to yourself, for heaven's sake. We'll talk about it as soon as we get the chance. I believe you.'

He believed about the suicide note not being one at all, but he didn't believe anything else. He went miserably with Parsons to his hard berth for the night. Head prefects had a room to themselves, with strictly one bed, and Parsons wouldn't even give him a pillow. He had been entertaining Jane Reeves and was more annoyed about the interruption than Jonathan.

'Get down on the floor where you belong, you raving twit, and if you snore I'll throw my shoes at you. Hard.'

'I don't snore.'

It was sisal matting and distinctly uncomfortable, but nothing like as uncomfortable as the train of thought Ashworth had set off in his brain. However much he had tried to forget that Hugo had been with Robinson and had lied about it, the fact had caused him a good deal of distress, and this new discovery was full of alarming implications. Just how alarming he hadn't had time to work out. The main thing was to stop Ashworth blabbing about it to anyone else before he had thought out what to do. It was a police thing really, but Jonathan couldn't face that. When Parsons was breathing heavily from the comfort of his well-sprung bed, Jonathan crawled across to the door and let himself out into the corridor, and went back to his room.

'Ashworth!'

Ashworth wasn't asleep either. His pudgy face in the half-darkness was still smudged with blood and his eyes were swollen.

'I'm sorry I hit you,' Jonathan said, 'That's not what I came to say though.'

'I'll bet,' said Ashworth.

'What do you mean by that?'

'I've been thinking – you can't always tell me what to do, Meredith –'

'You asked, Ashworth – "Only you can possibly decide" –'

'Well, it's different now.'

'How different?'

'We can't just ignore what I've found out. You want to, because of Hugo. You know it's bloody peculiar, don't you? Admit it.'

Jonathan wouldn't. 'What's the good of raking it all up?'

'Because otherwise I'm left carrying the can, making him commit suicide and all that. Apart from which, it's much too fishy to ignore. You know it is. First Hugo being down there that night and saying he wasn't, and now this.'

'How come it wasn't just Robin himself, seeing that what he'd written for your essay would do as a suicide note, tearing it out and leaving it on the table?'

'Because, if you are imminently intending to commit suicide, you're hardly likely to sit down first and correct some lousy sixth form essays, are you?'

True, Jonathan thought.

'I thought,' said Ashworth slowly, 'you could take the book to Hugo and show him, and ask him what he thinks.'

'You must be joking?'

'Why? You're very pally with him, aren't you? You've got a difficult problem, and you want some advice. What more natural than to ask him what he thinks you should do? He doesn't know you saw him down there that night, does he? If he's guilty, it'll show.'

'What do you mean, guilty?'

'Exactly what I say. You can't hide your head in the sand all the time, Meredith. It's all very peculiar. You just can't deny it. I bet the police would be interested, if they saw that page, and they knew Hugo was with Robin at ten o'clock that night.'

Jonathan felt despair, knowing that everything Ashworth was saying was, for once in a lifetime, accurate and sensible. Ashworth, indeed, seemed to have gained an extra dimension from somewhere, not exactly intelligence, but cunning. His face had a sly look, and Jonathan got the impression that he was enjoying the situation.

'What are you getting at exactly?'

'I've told you – ask Hugo and see what he says.'

'You don't mean it?'

'I do. I want you to show him the book, and say you think the page was taken as a suicide note when really it was just a comment on my essay, and what does he think you should do with the evidence.'

'And what if I say I won't?'

'I'll take the book to Armstrong in the morning.'

'Why?'

'Look, Meredith, I've told you. I don't think Robinson committed suicide. I want to find out. And you can

70

bloody well do the finding out. It's right up your street – you're always going to his cottage for little chats, aren't you? Well, go for another one tomorrow, and see what he says when he sees this book! Tell him you saw him down there and see what he says! Ask him what it's worth to keep quiet! I want to know – I can't wait, in fact –'

'You *swine* –' Jonathan stared out of the window into the bright blue summer night, picturing the confrontation. He felt as if the hard core of his body was melting, and lay back on his bed. He was trembling.

'You'll enjoy it,' Ashworth said. He was animated with malice, smiling.

Jonathan wanted to hit him, harder than before, but he had no strength. He got up and went back to Parsons's room and his bed on the floor and lay looking at the shapes of the moonlight through the trees, wondering what he was going to uncover. But it couldn't make him unhappier than Iris, could it? Whatever it was. Could it? It had been a very strange day.

CHAPTER
4

It wasn't any better, or nicer, in the morning. Jonathan
was going to see Hugo after supper, to sort out gear for
the trip to Wales.

'You must tell him then,' Ashworth said adamantly. 'I
mean it. There's only you going to the cottage, isn't
there?'

'Yes.'

'You must ask him.'

It was, somehow, as if Ashworth was tasting power
for the first time in his life. He was genuinely looking
forward to the evening, to forcing Jonathan into this
dreadful interview. 'Or else,' he said. Jonathan wasn't
sure if going to Mr Armstrong might be wiser. If Fletcher had sent him to Armstrong for his misdemeanour
the night before, he might have found the courage to say
something, but Fletcher merely gave him a grilling in
front of the class, and he was unable to put in any sort
of a defence, for Ashworth's particular provocation was
unrepeatable, indefensible. Jonathan lived in the op-
timistic hope that between the present time and evening
something would happen to prevent the confrontation,
but nothing did, and by supper-time his state of mind
was so perturbed that he began to want to get it over.

Ashworth was watching him from the next table with a sort of suppressed excitement – Jonathan thought glee was not too strong a word. 'Why don't you come too?' Jonathan had invited him, but Ashworth shook his head. There were hidden nastinesses in Ashworth that Jonathan hadn't divined before; why should the situation appear to delight him? Jonathan presumed that it was the heady unfamiliarity of being top-dog. He could well grow up to be a blackmailer of the nastiest kind.

'What's up with you?' Parsons asked him.

'Nothing's up.'

'If you want to be separated from Ashworth, it can be fixed for next term without any trouble.'

'You could put him with Iris Webster,' Murphy said.

Parsons laughed.

Jonathan said bitterly, 'What's Jane been telling you? Gossiping bitch. It's not me that has girls in my room in the evening.'

'With Ashworth, who wants a girl?'

They all laughed. Jonathan knew he couldn't win, and kept quiet. He would ask for a room on his own next term.

'Iris likes you, apparently,' Parsons said, watching him.

Roll on end of term, Jonathan thought, being careful to convey nothing. As if he didn't have enough on his plate!

When he had finished he fetched Ashworth's exercise book from their room, rolled it up and stuffed it in his back pocket, and set off for Hugo's cottage. Murphy and the others had gone to sort out the tents from the games pavilion, and count out tent-pegs and renew guy-ropes, and his job was merely to collect climbing-ropes and any ironmongery they might need and stow them ready in the school minibus. It had promised to be a pleasant evening, talking climbing to Hugo, excited about the coming trip and being able to savour it in the rope-scented armoury of Hugo's junk-room, sorting gear. But now all the pleasant anticipation had changed to anticipation of the grimmest kind. Jonathan walked slowly, scuffling up the dust and scowling, loathing Ashworth for his discovery. The evening was ruined before it had started.

Hugo was sitting at his dining-table writing reports.

'I'm sorry about this,' he said, 'but I've got to give them to the Head before we go, and there's only tonight. Only the Sixth form ones, so I shouldn't be too long, but you can get started. I've made a list – here –' He pushed it across the table. 'Make a pile by the front door and I'll fetch the bus when I'm through.'

Jonathan took it.

Hugo said, 'Something wrong?'

'No.' It was like going to the gallows, impossible to cover up. Hugo was smiling, cheerful, the table-lamp burnishing his features; he looked as if he, too, was as excited about Wales as Jonathan. He looked younger, somehow, and more animated than usual, more opened up and communicative. The very opposite from Jonathan's situation. Jonathan thought he must be imagining it. But Hugo smiled again and said, 'Been in trouble? I hear you've been behaving in a manner unfitting to prefectorial office –'

Thank God he didn't know why. Jonathan felt himself colouring up, and turned away in despair.

'You need a holiday, Meredith. I think we shall enjoy this trip. I'll be with you in twenty minutes.'

'Yes, sir.' He never called Hugo 'sir'.

He went into the other room and started on his task, working mechanically. The setting sun had gone behind the pine trees and it was gloomy, almost chill. He could feel the ridge of the exercise book in his back pocket riding over one of his scars, setting up an irritation, but he could not move it. It was his hair-shirt, his penance, for liking Hugo too well. He dreaded being let down. And he knew it was coming. Wasn't it? The worst thing he had ever done was see Hugo on the houseboat that night. And told Ashworth. *Ashworth* . . .

After what seemed a very long time, Hugo said, 'Do you want a beer?'

Jonathan didn't, but said, 'Please.'

He went into the other room and saw the reports neatly stacked, his own, presumably, amongst them. He stood looking at the tablecloth, listening to his heart beating, while Hugo fetched two cans of beer. He took one.

'This time tomorrow night – here's to our trip,' Hugo said, holding up the beer-can. 'We should have some lovely climbing if the weather stays like this – perfect conditions. Thank God for the end of term. Sometimes I'm not sure if school-mastering is my metier. Except that it pays you, unlike climbing.' He looked at Jonathan closely, hesitated. 'What's up with you, Meredith?'

Jonathan, watching a fly on the table, said, 'Something – I want to ask you –'

'What about? Serious?' His voice was unconcerned, but gentle. 'Sit down. Let's have it. Don't spoil anything, Meredith.'

'No.' It had only been Ashworth forcing him into it, once, but now it was more than that. He pulled out the exercise book and put it on the table, open at the last page. 'I don't know what to do,' he said. 'And it seemed better to show you . . . ask you . . . rather than anybody else.'

Hugo was looking at it reflectively, not showing surprise, or puzzlement. Not showing anything at all.

'I had to go to the inquest, and I saw the suicide note. And Ashworth's book was open on the table – he said Mrs. Robinson had brought them back, the ones he had been correcting the night he – he died –' His voice dried up.

Hugo waited, looking at the book. He looked at Jonathan. 'And?'

'You can see, the suicide note is that page torn out. It was a comment on Ashworth's essay, not a suicide note at all.'

Hugo said nothing. He sat down and looked at the book, reading the whole page down very carefully. His eyes moved across to the empty page opposite, and stared at it for a long time. His expression was completely blank.

Then he said, 'What am I supposed to say? Why have you brought it to me? Why not to Mr Armstrong?'

'Because you were there,' Jonathan said, agonized.

'What do you mean?'

Hugo, for a fraction of a second, looked very young, very startled, and completely unlike the revered Himalayan climber 'of immense physical and mental resource'.

'I saw you.'

'Christ, Meredith – !' The words whispered – did he hear them at all? – the eyes very wide, anguished, blue; then dropped to the exercise book, the eyelids shuttering down, the expression gone completely, the face immobile, stiff. Silence.

Jonathan, aware of a last thrust of the late sunshine through a gap in the pines, a flood of eerie light, dust-speckled, on a threadbare carpet, a pair of climbing boots all ready to go, shining and supple . . . lost, shattered, appalled.

Hugo then, clearing his throat, his face remote and cold – Himalayan – pushing the book back to Jonathan across the table: 'I can't advise you. You must do what you think best. Whatever you think . . . ' He paused, considered. 'No, that's not fair. I think, if you tell anybody, it should be Mr Armstrong. Either go to the top, or to no one at all. Tell him exactly what you think, if you wish. If it would please you. But it won't change anything, remember. It won't make anything any different, or any better. Not for Mrs Robinson, or for Robinson himself. Nor for you or me.'

'I know.'

The face colder still, a rock face, the eyes icy: 'I wasn't there, Meredith. You have made a mistake.'

Was he dreaming it? How could a face look like that, glittering? It was the light, the peculiar last light of the day, over polishing, making hysterical the concerned expression of the schoolmaster. Jonathan felt very cold, and slightly sick. He looked down at the table, and when he looked up again Hugo looked perfectly normal. Rather stern, as if the mathematics weren't going well. Not particularly affable, but normal enough.

'You've found everything on the list?'

'Everything except the guide – the book.'

'I'll find that.'

'Shall I go now?'

'Yes.'

He came to the front door with him. Jonathan rolled the exercise book up and stuck it in his back pocket again.

'Does anyone else know about it?' Hugo asked.

'No.' Lying was no prerogative of Hugo's, Jonathan thought heavily.

'Don't spoil Wales, Meredith. Go to Armstrong when we get back, if you must, but let's get our trip in first.'

But Wales was already spoilt.

He thought Hugo might say something more, and hesitated, but Hugo wasn't going to help him any more. Hugo was his usual reserved, uncommunicative self.

Jonathan walked away along the pine-needle path, head down, his mind blasted. What had he expected? He hadn't dared to think, hope, anything. And what had he found out? He still wasn't very sure. No comfort, which is what he supposed he had hoped for. He felt completely thrown, exhausted, as if he had come in from a long cross-country. He couldn't face going back to Ashworth, and stopped against one of the pines and leaned back on the warm trunk, wanting to get his mind working properly again. There was no hurry, all the time in the world. It was dusk now, and the smell of resin and pine-needles was friendly and familiar; the lights of Meddington were clustered away across the lawns and the tall chimneys reaching for the first star. Nothing was any different, after all. And Wales was tomorrow. Damn Hugo, for not being the Himalayan man, the rock, God Almighty . . . he had, for an instant, chickened out like a schoolboy, the pants scared off him . . . or had it been a trick of the light? His own over-active imagination working on the awful suspicions? What did Hugo think now? That he, Jonathan, was blackmailing him in some way? Why the hell hadn't he told Hugo that Ashworth was involved, Ashworth was the blackmailer? Because, when it came to the point, he wanted to know the truth even more badly than Ashworth.

But Ashworth, in his new power role, Jonathan could not stomach. He slithered down the trunk and sat down, stretching out his legs, deciding to wait until Ashworth would have flaked out, flabby and porcine in his winceyette pyjamas – for Ashworth was a tired mortal and slept readily. Jonathan decided to do an Iris Webster, curled up on the pine needles to get away from 'them', keep himself to himself, his miseries secret. Tomorrow, when he was fresh, he could pulverize Ashworth in his old style. Tonight, he wouldn't be able to find the words.

It then struck him that, if there was no exercise book, no proof, nothing to take to Armstrong, Ashworth would have no case. It would only be his word, raving, and he, Jonathan, would refute it, say the exercise book had never been. After all, as Hugo had so rightly said, producing this fresh evidence to the authorities wasn't going to change anything. It was altogether a mountain out of a molehill: Ashworth not wanting to have caused a suicide and then, by the nasty way his mind worked, finding he had a hold, a power, over Jonathan himself, and getting carried away by it. Jonathan decided to go and throw the exercise book in the river. He would do that, and tell Hugo, and everything would be O.K., even Wales.

He got up and started to walk towards the river. Something at the back of his mind kept telling him that it couldn't possibly be so easy. He walked very slowly, heading for the prick of light that was Robinson's houseboat, and the river. He would keep downstream of it and tear the exercise book up and throw it well out on the current. Or perhaps bury it in the mud on the bank, or amongst the reeds, where it would disintegrate. Thinking of the mechanics of destroying the book, the relatively simple thing, he knew he was keeping his mind off what it was working round to: the awful, ghastly question which he had kept under the whole time, like squashing the lid down on a jack-in-a-box, and that was now threatening to burst. If Robinson hadn't committed suicide, how had he died, and why?

Don't think about it.

There was someone walking along the river bank towards the houseboat.

Jonathan froze where he stood. The figure had come out from the darkness of the pines where Hugo's cottage was, and showed up clearly against the line of the riverbank. The lights of Hugo's cottage had gone out.

It must be Hugo. Jonathan didn't want it to be, but didn't see that it could possibly be anyone else. It looked like him, moving smoothly, not hurrying, but fast enough. Jonathan knew he was going to the houseboat. He would have given anything for it to have been different, even not to have seen the figure, but it was all done and happening and inevitable. Jonathan carried on towards the river, not even caring – hoping, perhaps – that the figure might see him, and ask him what he was doing, but the figure didn't see him. It went to the houseboat and went on board and disappeared.

Jonathan walked on and came to the river bank about fifty yards down from the houseboat, which is where he had intended, and stopped.

So what? Now it was as bad as it could be. As if he was having his face pushed into it, willy-nilly, his eyes forced open, the facts spelled out, everything he had tried not to think about. The houseboat lay very tranquil, the lights glowing through the windows in the hull, splashing across the smooth water. Jonathan wanted to see in, but couldn't. The boat was moored well out from the bank to its own piles, with a long gangplank spanning the gap, and from the bank one was too high up to see into the windows, which were only just above water-level. One needed to be right down low, which meant in the water.

Jonathan stood and thought about it for a bit. God was pushing him, he thought. It shouldn't have happened like this. It was not of his own doing. Hugo, I didn't mean it to be like this. But you've done it yourself. It was impossible to go away and leave it. He walked towards the houseboat slowly, an iron filing to a magnet. The water was cold, colder than one would have guessed from such a summer. He slithered in, holding the gang-plank, and it came up to his armpits, pulling at him hard. He wasn't sure, if he let go, whether he would be able to stand up against it, but he would have to try.

The window was some ten feet down from the gangplank. He put his hands on the hull for support, but silently . . . the water pressed him against painted wood; he had to brace himself, frightened of losing his footing. The buoyancy of his body was difficult to fight, the water up to his neck and only his flattened hands to keep himself in place, stopping himself from spinning off like a leaf on the current out of control. He inched his way down, taut with apprehension, his feet on the soft bottom every bit as precarious as on the folly. A light from the window splashed the metallic surface, cut off by his own head when he reached it. He braced his arm to stay still. He was shivering and sick with disgust at what he was doing, yet sicker still to *know* ... it was imperative now, having come so far. But he had to force himself to look, almost as if Ashworth's hand were on his neck, pressing him: it was a compulsion outside his own instincts.

And, looking, he felt no surprise. No shock. Merely a sense of inevitability, having known ... perhaps for quite a long time, if he had had the courage to admit it to himself. They were sitting together on a sofa and Hugo had his arms round Patsy. Her head was resting on his chest, turned into his body, and he had his cheek against her hair, and one hand stroking it gently. Perhaps she was crying, it was hard to tell. He was talking; Jonathan could see his lips moving. Telling her what had happened, he was sure, telling her about his visit, the exercise book ... 'Meredith knows ...'

And then, so careful up to now, losing concentration, his feet lost their grip and he went under, very suddenly, so that he got a throatful of water. He was underneath the flat bottom of the boat, the current bumping him, like being keel-hauled, unable to find open water. He groped up, his body twisting, clawing for release, strands of weed from the bottom of the boat sliding over his face and fingers, banners of slime. He was choked, drowning and wondering whether it mattered, panicking, yet one small part of him still apart in a state of horror for something quite other than what was happening to him: there was no point in fighting, somehow, as if it didn't depend on his own will at all, but only on a course of events over which he had no control. The current would either drown him or throw him clear; he had no choice in the matter. He reached up again, feeling it was the last time, and his hand surfaced, the black dark gave way to starlight and air to breathe. He heard himself coughing and hawking and knew he must keep quiet, but couldn't. He threshed out for the bank, desperate, caught a handful of reeds and held on, finding bottom with his knees. He was only, in spite of the aeons of time that seemed to have elapsed, thirty or so feet downstream of the boat, and the door had opened, throwing a shaft of light across the bank, so that he knew Hugo was investigating. He had certainly heard the body thudding along the bottom of the boat – had Robinson's done the same a week earlier? *Jeez!* – this was desperate! He would have done better to have floated on down, but too late to rethink now. He let out all his breath and eased himself down under the water, his head turned away from the boat, but sideways for a few mouthfuls of air, feeling the current bowing round him, forcing him, streaming him in its powerful direction, so that this knuckles whitened on the reed-roots. He could feel, hear, guess nothing, couching inanimate like a native of the river ooze. For all he knew Hugo was right there, looking down on him, at his black hair streaming and his white hand clutching. He had only to stamp on the hand, kick his face, thrust him away . . . he would drown, like Robinson, having no strength and no will-power, and all his secrets with him. A minute passed like a century, and he risked one eye, seeing nothing. With infinite caution he raised his head an inch or two and his released ears heard a voice, female:'. . . only a log. You get them like that . . .'

'Dreadful to be so jumpy – that's the worst thing, having a conscience for something that . . .' Hugo's voice, alarmingly close, drove Jonathan back under, petrified. His body throbbed to his drowning pulse, until he was forced to find air again, and the voices were farther away, but turned in his direction:

'. . . different complexion on it. But not to be *afraid*, Patsy, whatever happens. Morally there is no guilt, not when . . .'

The voice faded; he couldn't catch any more. They went back on the boat and stood on the deck, talking softly, and Jonathan shifted his numb grip in despair, feeling as if the cold swift water was in his bloodstream, his skin porous, his bones turned to cobweb. Even Ashworth, surely, hadn't wished this on him? But after about five minutes the door opened again and they went below, and Jonathan could hear only the fierce burbling of the water thrusting through the reeds and the chattering of his own teeth. He crawled up the bank and crouched still in the spiky grass, waiting to see if all was clear, then got up and ran, blundering through the lacy screens of willow and heading like a chased hare for the friendly lights of the school. He was in a distressed state, both physical and mental, and knew it, and after the initial couple of hundred yards he slowed down to try and sort things out a bit. One thing: he wasn't going back to his room and Ashworth. Ashworth was to be avoided at all costs until the departure for Wales, which was scheduled for after lunch the following day. Wales – that was another problem altogether, living with Hugo for two days with all those questions crackling unspoken between them like static electricity . . . Jonathan did not want to contemplate it. He squelched along the gravel path, unseeing, the wet jeans clamped to his legs . . .

'Meredith!'

It was Fletcher, taking his dog out for its nightly run, looming round the shrubbery where the path was narrow. He was accompanied by Miss Slater.

'What on earth – ?'

Jonathan could not answer; there was nothing he dared say. He stood, cornered, while the two teachers took in his no doubt extraordinary appearance – not to mention smell; there was nothing he could do other than push back the corkscrews of hair which were dripping monotonously over his forehead and remove a water-lily bud out of the neck of his clinging T-shirt.

'You've been in the river! God, boy, don't you know the rules in this place, after five years? Have you gone mad?' Fletcher, an explosive but kindly man, was startled by the apparition and let fly, but Miss Slater, more perceptive, said, "Are you all right? Have you had an accident?'

He shook his head, finding it difficult to speak.

'What were you doing?'

'I – I fell in –'

'Meredith, infants fall in rivers. Not sixth-formers, not *prefects* . . . it's the same with fighting. We had this conversation this morning, remember?'

'Oh, Jim, leave him. He's in a state. He's shivering,' Miss Slater said. 'You can talk to him later. He ought to go and get a hot bath.'

'Yes, get rid of that stink. You haven't been having another argument with Ashworth?'

'No.'

'Well, go and get cleaned up then, and come to my study before you go to bed.'

'Yes, sir.'

Jonathan fled, cursing himself for getting caught. He hadn't even been looking . . . It only needed Fletcher to say in the staff-room, 'Guess what, Meredith fell in the river last night – I found him dripping wet,' and Hugo would guess what he had been doing – spying on the houseboat. The events of the last hour were too awful to contemplate, and what the consequences were likely to be there was no way of knowing.

It was gone ten o'clock and no one was about. He went to the bathroom and lay in the bath for half an hour, wondering what to do. He wasn't going back to his room and he wasn't going to see Fletcher. He didn't want to see anybody. But he could hardly sleep in the bath all night. He realized he had no clothes to put on, except the stinking wet ones, so he wrapped himself in two of the school's skimpy bath-towels and padded down the corridor to Parsons's room and knocked on the door. Parsons was in bed, reading.

'Hey, Parsons, I want sanctuary. Can I sleep on your floor again? And borrow a pair of pyjamas?'

'You and Ashworth been fighting again?'

'No.'

'How come the bath towels?'

'My things are in my room and I'm avoiding Ashworth as a matter of principle.'

'Uncomfortable things, principles,' Parsons said, and threw him a pair of pyjamas out of a drawer, and pulled down a sleeping-bag from the top of his wardrobe. 'Make yourself at home.'

Parsons was all right, Jonathan thought gratefully, sliding down into the lovely dark privacy of the sleeping-bag. No questions, in spite of being agog. That was true friendship. He needed true friendship.

CHAPTER
5

'Parsons, Meredith isn't in his room. Do you know where he is?'

'He's in here, sir, asleep.'

'Oh. Good. I was worried . . . as long as he's . . . ' Fletcher yawned and sighed. 'He's behaving very strangely, but it can wait till morning. Good-night.'

'Good-night, sir.'

Long silence.

'You're not asleep, are you?'

'No. Thanks, Parsons.'

'Iris Webster was looking for you.'

That was all he needed.

Silence. All night to think about it. Hugo in love with Robinson's wife, murdering Robinson. Ashworth's joke diagnosis, after the inquest. True. *Impossible!* Hugo . . . calm, honest, fair, intelligent, courageous . . . *perfect* . . . a murderer. A perfect murderer. Nobody knew, suspected, save himself, and Ashworth. Hugo knew he knew. He didn't know about Ashworth. Ashworth mustn't say anything. The exercise book was missing, eased out of his back pocket by the current and by now a pappy indecipherable mess somewhere in the river: the vital evidence was destroyed. It was merely in the mind. All in the mind. And Ashworth needn't ever know the truth. He never saw Hugo's face, never saw the moment's panic in the steady, blue, mountaineering eyes, the horror, the wild pain at the consequences of discovery . . . did he ever see it himself, truly? Or was it a figment of the imagination? But Patsy in Hugo's arms was no figment of the imagination. And if Fletcher said anything about finding Meredith dripping wet with water-lilies in his hair at ten o'clock in the evening, Hugo would know that he had seen him with Patsy . . . Jonathan, adrift in the storm of his own anguish, never knew whether he slept or not, remembered only crawling into his own room sometime around dawn to collect his clothes while Ashworth still slept, then oblivion for an hour until Parsons stirred him with a foot and said, 'Action, Meredith. Morning is broken and all that rot.'

He awoke to an instinctive conviction that his world was quite destroyed, before he even remembered all that had happened. Remembering, he knew that one's instincts were pretty reliable, and opened his eyes bleakly to what should have been one of the best days of his life.

'You're off on this Wales lark at lunch-time, is that right?' Parsons was standing at the window shaving with an electric razor. 'Looks like the weather is breaking.'

The room was grey and hot.

'Thunderstorms, I'd say. Just your luck, eh?'

'Luck's not my thing lately.'

'Poor boy. I can see you get shot of Ashworth next year, if that's any consolation. You're on the short-list for house-prefect, so you might get in here if you're lucky.'

Jonathan didn't call being made house-prefect lucky, any more than he found it possible to look forward to next term. Hard even to see his way through to lunch-time, avoiding all the people he particularly did not wish to meet. Hard to see beyond that, too. Not to think . . .

'Fletcher thinks you're behaving very strangely. So do I.'

'Yeah. Bad material for a house-prefect.'

How could he avoid Ashworth at breakfast? Avoid breakfast. But he was starving. He went down, avoided Fletcher by making a detour round the main hall and coming in by the french windows conveniently near to the prefects' table. Ashworth was late for breakfast – naturally, having no one to wake him up, but Hugo was eating as usual, sitting next to Fletcher. Suppose Fletcher said, at the breakfast table, 'I saw Meredith last night . . . '? But Linda Slater was sitting opposite Fletcher, cool and smart. Fletcher might not want to admit walking in the grounds at night with Miss Slater, perhaps better not to say anything. Jonathan, watching, saw nothing to indicate that Fletcher had remembered the events of the night before, nor Hugo either. If they all determined to ignore them, him too, then perhaps there was no problem, nothing to worry about? Nothing had ever happened? Hugo had finished and was leaving. Fletcher was on his last cup of tea. Danger almost passed. The door opened and Ashworth came in, very late, finding the dishes almost empty. Jonathan crammed in the last of his toast and marmalade. Ashworth looking round . . . angry . . .

'Hey, Meredith, where did you get to –?'

Jonathan pushed back his plate and stood up.

'I want to talk to you, you rat,' Ashworth said heavily.

'No fighting, no brandishing of cutlery, Ashworth,' Parsons said lightly. 'Go to your menial table like a good lad, and leave your betters in peace.'

'Meredith, I want to talk to you. Now.' It was Fletcher, appearing like *deus ex machina*. 'Come with me.'

Ashworth glowered at them both. Parsons murmured, 'How the boy is in demand!'

Jonathan went with Fletcher, too numb to work out a defence, unable to think.

'I'm disappointed in you, Meredith. We've made you house-prefect for next year, and you're one of three possibles for head boy, and yet all of a sudden you're behaving like an imbecile. What's got into you? Is there any explanation you want to offer?'

'No, sir.' What if he were to say, 'Yes, sir. Mr Hugo is a murderer and an adulterer and his behaviour is upsetting me.'?

'You can talk to me, you know that.'

Not about this he couldn't.

'It's all right, sir. I'm sorry.'

'So am I. If you would talk things over – we've had all this with you before, haven't we? – it makes life easier, in a community like this. We have to live as a community. You are far too private a person for your own good.'

No possible answer. Don't attempt one.

'I have to nag you, Meredith, although I would rather not. We are giving you a position of responsibility for your own good. I hope you will appreciate it. I doubt it, actually, but you should know we mean well. I am saying this now as I know you are off to Wales with Mr Hugo, and I might not have another chance before the end of term. You'll be back Friday?'

'Friday night, sir.'

'I thought so. And as we break up on Saturday, I might not see you again. Oh – the other bit of briefing, about Saturday. You're to read the lesson in assembly. You've managed to avoid it with one excuse or another the whole year, but it's caught up with you at last. So remember to sit by the platform without being reminded.'

'Yes, sir.' The least of his worries.

'And if, when you are in Wales, you find an opportunity to talk any difficulties over with Mr Hugo – I know you get on well with him – you possibly have more affinity with him than you do with me – take the opportunity, Meredith. I'm sure you will find him sympathetic. It always helps to have a little discussion.'

'Yes, sir,' – faintly, the mind reeling. I've already done so. I've already discussed with him my discovery that he is a murderer.

'Are you all right, Meredith?'

'Yes, sir.'

'I think you need a holiday. Have a good time in Wales then. And bear in mind what I've said.'

'Yes, sir. Thank you.'

He fled, wits reeling, and locked himself in the lavatory until Ashworth should have gone to lessons, then he went to his room and packed his rucksack for the climbing trip and took it outside and loaded it into the bus that was parked on the front drive. He went to lessons, his mind a blank, and avoided Ashworth at lunchtime by getting his dinner straight from the kitchen and eating it in the freezer room. By then it was almost departure time. He checked his watch with the kitchen clock and made his way to the bus. Murphy and Pettifer and Franklin were sitting on the front steps, so if he joined them he would be safe from any likely last-minute approach from Ashworth. He turned in their direction, but was interrupted by a breathless summons and running footsteps from behind.

'Jonathan!'

It was Iris, jangling across the lawn, having detached herself from a group of surprised females who were all staring. Jonathan, very much aware that Murphy and co. were also agog, stopped angrily, heart plummetting.

'Are you going now?'

'Yes.'

'I wanted – wanted to speak to you.' She became aware of the boys smirking on the steps, and Jonathan's embarrassment, and went scarlet. It occurred to Jonathan then that she must be quite desperate to have approached him in this way, and to have called him by his

Christian name. He tried not to be annoyed, keeping the irritation out of his voice.

'What is it?'

She was mortified, close to tears. 'I'm sorry,' she said. 'It doesn't matter –'

'No, truly. I'm only hanging around, until we go.' He was terrified she was going to burst into tears. 'Is anything wrong?'

'Oh – no, please –' Her face was white as chalk and the tears brimming. 'I shouldn't have – I didn't realize – just to say good-bye –'

'It's only two days. I'll be back for breaking-up.'

'No. it's not that really. I just thought there might be time to talk, but I shouldn't have – I've done everything wrong again. I'm sorry.'

'There's nothing to be sorry for –' more gently; she looked awful.

'My mother's written, to say she can't collect me until after the week-end. I've got to stay here. She's got a concert – she'd *forgotten* to say –' Her face was agonized.

Jonathan was amazed. 'She *can't* –'

'No – I can't bear it –'

It was first aid again, really, Jonathan thought desperately – but impossible . . . Hugo was coming down the steps with the rest of the party.

'Iris, I'm sorry – oh, blast it! Look, don't be upset – it will sort itself out all right, I'm sure. I'll come and see you when I get back –'

What was he saying? Who was he to give comfort, when he needed help even more badly than she did? She was appealing to him as desperately as he needed to appeal to some unlikely God to see him out of his own mess, and with as little chance of comfort. He felt close to bursting into tears himself and weeping with her, but with a monumental effort he kept himself calm, even diffident, and smiled and said, 'I'm sure you can go home with someone else for a day or two – with me, if you like, until your mother's free –'

'I'm *sorry* –' she said blindly. She was crying now.

'No, don't. Don't! I've got to go –'

There was a toot from the van. He turned and ran, flinging himself into the open door as the engine started up. He felt completely steam-rollered, flattened under these unaccustomed emotions, assailed from all quarters.

'Cripes, she's *crying* 'cause you're leaving her, Meredith!'

'Oh, Jonathan, I can't bear it!' – in a high falsetto, collapsing into mirth.

'Don't fall off, darling – I can't live without you!'

It was awful, as bad as anything for a long time, everything coming at him all at once.

'Climb through into the front beside me, Meredith,' Hugo said over his shoulder. 'I want a navigator I can trust. The rest of you are behaving like third form dimwits. If that's to be the standard for the rest of the trip I'm not encouraged.'

Jonathan went gratefully, bitterly angry.

'The map's in the glove locker. We want the M6. Work it out.' Jonathan was sure that Hugo knew the way to North Wales blindfolded, but groped about for the map, while the others sorted themselves out, still exploding with laughter.

'It's nothing to do with me, her crying. She's in trouble about something,' he muttered, hating Hugo to think –

'Pregnant,' Murphy said.

Howls of laughter.

Hugo slowed down and drove at about fifteen miles an hour until the passengers in the back took the hint and quietened down.

'Why are we going so slowly, sir?'

'Give you time to grow up.'

'Oh, *sir* –!'

It gradually sorted itself out, normality returning,

Jonathan released from his terrible shame, not wanting to think about it, determined not to . . . as if he didn't have enough! Six hours of Hugo at his side, to talk to as if nothing had happened. He was in such a state he could easily believe that, in fact, he had merely been imagining things last night, that none of it had happened. Hugo was quite unchanged, not hostile, not bad-tempered, inviting his company, sympathetic, driving without any sort of tension. I must forget it for the next two days, Jonathan thought, otherwise it will be quite impossible. Think about it on the drive back, and decide then. Switch off. Think climbing. He slumped back in his seat, watching the country fly past. He felt exhausted.

'I'm picking up a friend in Betws-y-Coed,' Hugo said. 'He's down from Oxford, climbing, and willing to help out for a couple of days. It will give you all more turns on the harder climbs. The first day, I thought, we'll do a round walk, perhaps a bit of easy climbing and some practice in navigation, compass work and all that, and the second day just climbing – extend you a bit on the real thing, see what you can achieve. Pity time's so short, but it's better than nothing at all.'

Jonathan navigated meticulously, finding the M6 without getting bogged down in Leamington or Coventry and gazing dumbly out over the lunaresque rooftops of the Birmingham environs with his usual feeling of unease and pity for what had been done in the name of progress – progress being the vital achievement, for the Volkswagen bus was cruising at sixty-five without effort.

'Exit twelve,' he said. 'For Shrewsbury. Is that what you want?'

'Yes.'

The weather was grey and close and visibility bad. The air smelled of thunder.

'What time d'you think we'll be there?' Pettifer asked.

Hugo glanced at his watch.

'Eightish, with luck. In time to make camp before dark anyway.'

'Where are we camping?'

'I thought Cwm Silyn would suit us. It's on the far side of Snowdon. Two lakes and some nice climbing handy, and we can take the bus almost all the way. There's a hard track.'

Jonathan, as the hours passed, lapsed into a state of acceptance of what had happened which he thought would see him through the next two days. It was as if some kind of natural anaesthesia had spread across the disturbed part of his thinking, a numbness of the emotions. He felt very tired, and without excitement or anticipation of any kind. He could not hide this feeling, and his companions made solicitous remarks about his lack of response to their high spirits, putting it down to pining for Iris. He accepted this without even feeling angry. He would not think about Iris: she was altogether outside his capabilities. He watched the country turning gradually into Wales, rolling and lonely and grey, and Hugo, with dawdling tourist cars and caravans to pass, was silent. Jonathan glanced at him once or twice, convinced that his change in his conception of the man must show, somehow, but nothing was different in appearances; Hugo was still easy, patient, apparently unperturbed. Between them, Jonathan realized, they would work out this extraordinary charade of nothing having happened. But when they got back to school . . . no, switch off, time enough later. Blank.

They picked up the friend in Betws-y-Coed, an amiable, chatty young man in well-worn climbing breeches and tattered anorak. Jonathan climbed over into the back and concentrated on fishing his old jersey out of his rucksack and changing it for his blazer, pulling off his tie and stuffing it away, for he had never had the opportunity to change. The others had got tired of their ragging, but Murphy said, 'What's eating you, Meredith?', the question dropping into a chance silence for everyone to hear. Jonathan knew Hugo had heard it. 'Nothing,' he said. 'I've got a headache.' And the bus swayed and swooped its way down the winding road to Capel Curig and then out on to the moorland with Snowdon's great purple bulk looming in the grey evening ahead of them, ominous. Jonathan stared out of the window. They passed Pen-y-Gwryd, the famous old climbing inn, and took the road for Beddgelert, climbing up, winding, the dun sides of the mountains sheering up out of tangled forests and disappearing into low cloud. Slate-coloured water flattened out below on the valley floor.

'Right at Beddgelert, then left past the lake.'

There was a turning up past a white stone cottage into a bleak slate-scattered valley, empty and deserted in the cold evening, sheep bleating like lost souls, a sad, gone-away valley, narrow, steep and bare. It suits me, Jonathan thought. But they drove on down, past a lake, out into a scattering of houses and then, suddenly, left on to a track, and into low gear, climbing and winding and jolting, through an iron gate, and the stone walls were left behind, the track curving on across bare, shorn grass. Ahead of them terraces of black rock started to come into view over the near horizon, stark against the darkening sky.

The camp-site was impressive: Jonathan felt his heart lift in spite of everything, taking in the amphitheatre of the mountain curving round with two lakes in its claw, the water dark as slate. From the farther shore fans of scree reached up to the great slabs of climbing rock: the real thing, the object of the expedition. He stood taking it in, realizing how terribly urban the Meddington folly was by comparison. It was a lonely, dramatic place, stirred only by a chill wind making patterns across the lakes and the evening cry of a curlew drifting over the top crags. He carried his load up from the parked van and dumped it and walked on alone, and stood looking to where the track zig-zagged, white, to and fro across the scree slope to the foot of the rock walls. It was almost unbearable, the feel of having everything he wanted in his hands, like the lakes lying in the palm of the mountain's hand, and the whole thing nullified by this awful thing that had happened. Everything he had dreamed of – he was looking at it now, and his feelings were numb. He went back, and they made camp, and a meal, and got organized, and in the general hubbub and excitement his silence went unremarked. He had a two-man tent to share with Murphy; Hugo and his companion, Alan, were in another two-man, and the others had a larger tent out of the school stores. By the time they were all in their sleeping-bags and the torches extinguished, it was dark and, after only a few minutes of banter and skirmish, the camp fell silent. Jonathan, exhausted by the day's troubles, slept almost immediately.

It was hard to work out, afterwards, when he first began to feel afraid. Perhaps only after the shock of his discoveries began to wear off and his own intelligence took over once more, awakening from the cocaine state it had taken refuge in, perhaps alerted by the very subtle hardening in Hugo's attitude towards him: he became aware of Hugo singling him out, marking him, watching him, not in the protective way he had shown after the Iris embarrassment but with what Jonathan could only recognize as hostility. Or was it his own new feeling of hostility towards Hugo that was colouring his judgement? It was impossible to know, then or in retrospect, what the true situation was between them, for it was all guesswork, no emotions revealed, no words spoken, but just as impossible not to realize – once the mind was out of shock – that he, Jonathan, was now a considerable impediment to Hugo's future serenity. If I were Hugo, what would I be thinking, Jonathan kept wondering? And it occurred to him that Hugo's cool

courage, his intelligence, his resourcefulness and his im-
perturbability – all the characteristics that he had so
much admired – added up to a formidable adversary.
And adversary was the role Jonathan now saw him in,
not having willed it that way . . . no, he willed nothing,
but, having set the events in motion, the consequences
were snowballing on him. All he longed for now was the
end of term, home and oblivion. Mummy, in fact. Jeez,
what a state to have arrived at!

It was on the knife-sharp ridge of Crib Goch, jostled
by Murphy, looking down several hundred feet of sheer
rock which he had managed to avoid descending the
quick way, that he realized how useful for Hugo, if he
had gone. A quick, clean accident – and they were common enough in Snowdonia to arouse little excitement –
and Hugo's worries would be over. As, indeed, would
his. Jonathan trod more carefully, sobered by the
thought. Imagination again . . . as if he would . . . But he
had. Hadn't he?

It had rained all night and the rocks of Cwm Silyn in
the thin morning drizzle had been unsuited for novice
climbing, so Hugo had proposed a walk over Snowdon
and down by Crib Goch to Pen-y-Pass, where Alan
came round to meet them in the minibus. They had
done compass and map work, discovered how easily
one lost one's sense of direction in low cloud, enjoyed
some breath-taking panoramas from the ridge walk and
fallen into the café at the bottom as if they had been
away from food for a week. The fug of cooking mingled
amenably with the fug of damp, sweaty bodies and
warm steaming woollies; Jonathan, sitting down with a
cup of tea, felt the sharpness of salt sweat on his tongue,
felt the cold drops of moisture falling off the corkscrew
ends of his forelock and savoured the physical relief
with real pleasure. He liked the feeling of pushing his
body, stretching it; there was too much of sitting and
pen-pushing in his life, not enough physical exhaustion.
That was what he liked the horses for, at home, not

hunting and racing because it was smart, but because it jerked the poor white body out of its central heating and made it aware of the real nature of things. Now, with his cup of tea, he knew –

'You could be fitter, eh?' Hugo brought his tea to the seat opposite. 'It brings it home to you.'

'I was thinking that, yes.'

'And yet we're probably fitter than eighty-five per cent of the people in this country. It's a pity Meddington, with all its privilege, couldn't buy up Snowdonia and park it in the grounds.'

'Suggest it to Armstrong.'

'It would look good on the prospectus.'

They both grinned, the old compatibility asserting itself, blotting out the strain. Yet, strangely, this was worse than anything. Jonathan felt a lump come into his throat.

'We can do a spot of climbing when we get back,' Hugo said. 'Nothing difficult, just to get the feel of it. Then, if it's dry tomorrow, we'll spend the day there.'

'On that big slab?'

'I'll take you on something that will extend you, if that's what you want. Something nice and exposed. The Outside Edge, perhaps.'

'What grade is that?'

'It's a hard Very Difficult.'

'What about the others?'

'No. They aren't ready for it.'

Jonathan, granted the privilege, felt exposed already, even in the café. Nervous? Jeez, it was what he wanted, wasn't it? Hugo was looking at him, smiling. Jonathan tried to read his expression, wondering if he was hiding his own turmoil from the clear blue eyes . . . but there was no malice, no aggro. Kindness, he would have said, sympathy certainly. The warmth, the tea, the sausages and chips were bringing back normality. Had it ever been any different? God, what a chaos his mind was in! He was beyond sorting it out. He would have to rely on instinct, like an animal. It was terribly wearing. He felt like a hundred and ten.

They went back and spent the evening learning about belays on real rock with jammed nuts and slings, and trying them out on some easy rocks Hugo found them after another short journey by minibus. The weather had cleared up and the rocks were dry. By the time they got back and were walking the last lap down the track it was going dusk and the clouds, relenting, had rolled away to show all the tops sharp and hard against the sky. The stars, reflected in the lakes, lay in the hollow like a great field of daisies. For all it was high summer, it smelled cold and primeval and stark with the coming of darkness and Jonathan knew that, for all its tourists and climbers in orange anoraks, and chips and hot coffee on Pen-y-Pass, it was unchanged and oblivious and impervious and had been so since the Ice Age, and would remain so, unmoved. The frothy, tiny tide of human activity that assailed it by day was infinitesimal by these standards, his own troubles a pinhead in a galaxy. But the sane perspective was no help. He slept badly and went out for comfort to gaze on the black circling arm of the mountain under the stars, padding barefoot over the cold dewy grass to the edge of the lake. The silence was as pure and refreshing as the water at his feet, away from the sullen flapping of the tent and heavy breathing of his unconscious companions; the stars were sharp, a great strewing of brilliants across the crags like seeds from the hand of a heavenly broadcaster, some growing strong, some faint and barely rooted, all of them greater than his own planet and greater and older than the ancient rocks he stood on, and all of them putting him in his place, shrivelling his ego, mocking his small pretensions. But hardly bringing comfort, for all he wanted it . . .

A firefly light on a rock behind him caught his eye as he turned back, and he stared, trying to work out what it was. A figure sat there, as motionless as he had stood a moment ago, smoking a cigarette, looking at the mountain. It was Hugo. Jonathan supposed he was surprised, but wasn't, knowing only too well the feeling that had prompted him to take to the contemplation of nature. Had he seen him? Impossible to say. He wasn't facing his way. Jonathan had a pee, to make a reason for his excursion, and went back to the tent, having achieved nothing, save cold feet.

In the morning the clouds had come down again and even the top of Cwm Silyn was invisible. But it wasn't raining.

'We can climb,' Hugo said. 'The rock is dry, so far.'

They went back to the bus and got out the climbing gear, the ropes and ironware and helmets, and Hugo sorted it out and gave them a belt each and a rope between two and an assortment of slings and nuts. He said nothing to Jonathan about climbing the Very Difficult that he had mentioned the evening before. They took the gear back to camp, collected some bread and cheese and the thermoses they had prepared at breakfast time and set off up the scree. The others were excited and larking about, sending off showers of stones, but Jonathan climbed in silence, following Hugo, steadily and without effort. The air was grey and still and they were in mist before they had reached the top of the scree. Alan led the way, traversing over rough stones and wiry grass, and Jonathan thought the Great Slab was farther to their right, but didn't say anything. They came out on to some tussocky terraces, and steep, jumbled rock sheared up into the mist. Alan stopped.

'O.K. here?'

'Fine.'

It was nothing like the folly. It wasn't very difficult, but it was real, and the belays had to be done properly. Jonathan had to lead Pettifer, and make belays good enough to hold him, and was very much aware of being unprotected himself.

100

'If you come off it won't kill you, but it could be highly unpleasant,' Hugo said, which Jonathan could see for himself.

They learned more in a couple of hours than in weeks on the folly. Having led three times, and done well, and feeling pleased with himself, Jonathan was taking a swig from his thermos when Hugo said to Alan, 'I'm going to take Meredith to do one of the routes on the Great Slab. I promised him a good one. If you have lunch here now, and do an hour or two more, we'll see you down at the camp –' he glanced at his watch –' say, there o'clock?'

'O.K.'

It was very casual. Hugo slipped one of the coiled ropes over his shoulder and nodded at Jonathan.

'Coming?'

Jonathan returned the thermos to his rucksack, wriggled it on to his shoulders and followed without a word. He felt keyed-up, but did not want to *think*. It would do for him. Play it by ear, he thought, by instinct, like an animal. They moved together across the scree and through the streamers of mist, the ragged edges of the cloud, not talking. Hugo moved very easily, strolling, his hands resting in his pockets. They started to climb, and the rocks grew steeper on their left, and smoother, and altogether more businesslike. The lakes glimmered through the mist below, shining like two suns through a water-colour wash, all the details lost, the camp hard to define. It looked very far away and tiny. They went on climbing and came at last to a place where the rock towered up, disappearing into thick cloud, and even the scree they stood on sheered away steeply.

Hugo stopped and looked up. 'Two hundred and fifty feet,' he said. 'I'll lead, but you'll do it on your own, no help from the rope. You can take your time. It starts here. The first pitch is about sixty feet, and don't start climbing till you get the word from me.'

He dropped the rope coil at the foot of the rock and watched as Jonathan took the end and tied himself on

101

with a figure-of-eight knot through the two karabiners on the belt. He then tied himself on to the other end.

'The hardest part is on the second pitch, a bulge out to your left and bit of a traverse, where the rope isn't going to stop you all that kindly if you come off. It's very exposed, but it's good, clean climbing. We'll leave the rucksacks here. No point in cluttering ourselves unnecessarily.'

They propped them tidily against the rock. There was nobody in sight, either above or below, and no sound of any living creature, not even a sheep. They could have been on the moon, Jonathan thought. He didn't know whether he was frightened or not, the numbness having returned.

'I'll be off then.'

Jonathan watched, to see where he had to follow, but didn't see that he could possibly remember what he saw. Soon there wasn't anything to see anyway, save the rope jerking out spasmodically over the rock above and the rock disappearing into the murk. He was on his own. He waited. Not very long. But how long would it take him?

The spare rope was pulled up and came tight on his belt.

'That's me!' he shouted up.

He waited for the signal to climb, searching out the first holds, impatient. Hugo's voice floated down.

'Climbing!' he shouted in reply.

He had thought it looked fairly easy while he was waiting, but it wasn't, after the first ten feet or so. The holds were small and always seemed to be for the wrong foot, or miles out of reach, and he seemed to spend ages merely clinging and searching, not moving at all, muttering and groping, standing on a quarter of an inch wrinkle and holding with a finger-nail. The other hand and foot reached and searched and tested, and then the brain had to decide whether it was safe to transfer, and the higher he got the more the decision mattered.

It shouldn't have mattered, being second on the rope, but the instinct he had decided to rely on told him that it did; instinct was telling him that he was a fool to be doing this, putting his life into the hands of a man who would prefer him dead. He was sweating when he came up to Hugo's stance, but not with exertion.

'The crux comes in the next pitch. There's a traverse out to that bulge up there – it's awkward, you'll find. I'll put a runner in as I go across . . . Belay yourself on here.'

Hugo was cool and distant. His face was pale but sweat gleamed on his forehead. Jonathan said nothing. They moved round each other carefully on the small stance, Hugo watching as Jonathan made his belay.

'That's right. Now round your waist – that's it. After I've put the runner in, the pull would come from above, remember, if I were to come off. Before the runner, from below.' His voice was expressionless, the teacher's voice, automatic. Jonathan nodded. Hugo started to climb. The rope trailed out behind him, an orange loop across the hard slabs, moving steadily across the face to where the crucial bulge made a dark outline against the misty nothing beyond. He went round it and disappeared. The rope kept on running out. Jonathan waited. He was cold and shivers kept going through him, chattering his teeth. His mind was a blank. The rope stopped. He waited.

'Taking in!'

The voice drifted down the cliff. The spare rope uncoiled from Jonathan's feet, snaking up through the runner and over the bulge until it came tight on Jonathan.

Then, 'Come on!'

Jonathan acknowledged, and undid the belay. Instinct was getting the better of him, and he was glad to start. It was the same as before, groping and grunting and finding nothing: harder, colder and more difficult. He got to the running belay and released the rope from the karabiner. It fell away across the traverse. He could see himself coming off and penduluming out into the awful space below the bulge. He didn't think the rope was of any use to him at all; he didn't even believe it was belayed above. He stood on the rock, holding on by his finger-tips in tiny grooves, looking across to where he was supposed to go, looking down for footholds and seeing nothing but a sheer drop below to the scree, where the red rucksacks lay like bloodstains some seventy feet below and the whole mountain fell away in rivers of scree to the lakes and the pinprick tents. Beyond the valley floor the sea was breaking in white rollers over the Menai bar and the whole of Anglesey lay sprawled like a lilac cloak over the colourless water, horizon and sky merging beyond in a watery sun-shot haze. But Jonathan, spidered out on the rock wall, was not concerned with the scenery, only with finding his way. He could see a handhold, enormous, beautiful, but way out of reach, and his feet were all wrong, the right one needing to get out from under and the left one blocking the way. He was getting breathless, searching, his holds so insecure and the bloody rope, if he could spare a hand to test it – he was sure it was no more holding him than it was holding a seagull that drifted below on unmoving, outstretched wings . . . God, what a place to go! . . . a parachute wouldn't have been out of place . . .

He heard the stone coming from way up, and knew what it was without needing it spelled out.

He pressed himself against the wall, feeling his ankles trembling, the metallic scrape of his helmet on the rock. Shut his eyes . . . cling like a limpet . . . the stone hit the rock above him and sang out into space, whistling, falling clear, as a body would have fallen, and plunging down until it hit the scree with a crack that echoed all round the cwm. Jonathan, trembling, changed his foothold by act of God and reached up for the crucial handhold, scraping his body across the face. It had only needed the passing wind of that stone an inch or two nearer and he would have followed it down, splayed

104

and twisting and – unlike the seagull – finding no thermals to hold him. Jeez, could he ever believe it fell by accident? What was he doing here? The sweat of fear clammed on his body like a wet shroud. He struggled and grunted and inched his way to the stance and found Hugo waiting, the belay sound, the rope taut round his body, all in order.

He homed on to the ledge and stood up.

'That stone –'

'I heard it coming,' Hugo said. 'I shouted.'

'No.'

'A sheep up on the top. It's common enough. That's what the helmet's for. Here's your next belay.'

Nothing to be said. Hugo was cool, methodical, working like a machine, climbing like a fly. But Jonathan could not relate to him any more, could not bring himself to believe that this was an ordinary climb. If he was relying on instinct, instinct was clamouring to get off this mountain, to get on to the great safe hullocks of sheep-grazed grass that lay beyond the crags, to find some boisterous Youth Hostel kids in bright anoraks to gang up with, to get back to the valley. But it was impossible. He was alone in space, roped to a murderer, and they were climbing in cloud now, the valley disappearing below the wraiths of mist. If anything were to happen to him, no one would ever know how. Easy for Hugo, easy as falling off a log, or a rock. Nobody to see, nobody to say. He waited, watching the rope snake up into the cloud. Even easier for him, he supposed, were he to give the rope a sharp tug . . . but he had no good reason, as Hugo had good reason . . .

Instinct, Jonathan decided, was for animals. It was doing him no good at all. Humans used intellect to solve their problems. He waited, using intellect, calming himself down. Hugo belayed himself and called down to him; he unfastened his belay and started climbing again, concentrating on climbing well and not on getting pushed off. It improved things quite a lot; either the climbing was slightly easier, or he was gaining confidence, but it did not come so hard now: his movements were better controlled. It was because he was using his intelligence instead of his instinct. God, what an idiot he was! He could scare himself into making mistakes without any help from Hugo, if he did not concentrate on the job in hand, but let his mind wander like a hysterical child's.

The next stance was wide and grassy, suggesting that the climb was running out. They were in the clouds and the feeling of exposure was less, cocooned from the view, a world of their own. Hugo went on, saying nothing, and Jonathan waited, cool now, and very aware of his danger, but in a detached, intellectual way. That he could overcome his panics pleased him. But if he started thinking about falling stones . . . no – he was only thinking about climbing, looking for the route, remembering the techniques, keeping a nice balance. He followed up quite quickly. The next pitch was the last. When he came to the top he saw that the rocks had given way to tumbled terraces, steep but easy, with tracks and sheep-paths wriggling through boulders into the mist.

'We can unrope here,' Hugo said. 'That's it.'

Could it be? Trial by rock-face . . . was it over? Jonathan realized that he felt nothing but relief, no sense of achievement at all. There was no view, only the close, drifting cloud hemming them round, and the black rocks falling away beneath their feet into the void.

'Let me have the rope,' Hugo said.

Jonathan undid the knot and pulled it free. Hugo was standing right in front of him. With the rope dropping out of the karabiner, Jonathan instantly *knew* – two hundred and fifty feet to the scree below . . .

'No,' he said – whispered, agonized – 'It's not *fair* –'

Afterwards, it struck him as a ridiculous thing to have said.

Hugo was standing slightly above him, the rope still

on his belt but Jonathan's end dropped on the coil at his feet. He had both hands lifted, one foot braced back.

'No –?' Hugo repeated the word, with the slightest of questions in his voice. He was white to the lips. 'Why, Meredith, why did – Oh, Jesus, why does it have to be you, of them all?'

Jonathan wasn't sure if he heard correctly. And anyway, it didn't make sense. He stood, feeling his whole body trembling, petrified, feeling the whole of the two hundred and fifty feet below him, and remembering the stone, and the seagull, and his vision of a body falling, and Hugo's freedom if he went. He was sure then that it was all up with him. Knowing that he should drop to his knees and hold on tightly to solid rock, he straightened up instead and perversely defied Hugo, his soul already flung into the ether and all the angels waiting to gather him up, the way he felt. What showed in his face he would never know, but Hugo's resolve slowly, but quite visibly, caved in. The manic look gave way to despair, and then blankness. He dropped his hands and started to undo the end of the rope from his belt. Jonathan watched him. He could not speak, his lips were too dry. Hugo coiled the rope tidily, fastened it off and slung it over his shoulder. He was still very pale, his face drawn in a curious way. He looked to Jonathan quite old, suddenly, almost a stranger.

He said very quietly, 'We'll go and join the others.'

He turned round and walked on, to go over the brow of the mountain and find the path down the scree. Jonathan followed not sure if he was dreaming, not sure of anything at all. He followed him unthinkingly, scrambling wearily over the moonscape boulders and shorn grass. He wasn't sure what had happened. He was so jumpy he was dreaming things. Oh God, let me get home, he kept thinking, over and over again. I'm going bonkers. They'll put me in a home. There was nothing to be seen in the cloud save Hugo's figure in front of him, moving in its familiar, easy way, silent, unmoved.

He never said a word all the way down. Jonathan slid after him down the steep scree through the cloud, dropping and skidding and stumbling, not sure sometimes if the sweat wasn't tears, not sure of anything at all. By the time they got to the bottom Hugo was well ahead and Jonathan finished alone, plodding over the grass to the camp where the others had started to pack up.

Alan looked up from dismantling his tent.

He smiled. 'I hear you did the Outside Edge?'

'Yes.' Was that it?

'Very good for starters.' Alan dropped the metal tent-pegs into their bag and pulled the drawstring tight. 'You must be feeling pleased.'

'Yes.'

'Two girls got killed off that one some time ago. Very nasty.'

Jonathan sat down quickly on a handy pile of sleeping-bags and started to unlace his boots, his vision blurred, fingers like blotting-paper. He could hear the others laughing and larking about. He thought he was going mad.

CHAPTER

6

After the minibus had departed for Wales, Iris went to her room, threw herself on the bed and sobbed bitterly. Not only was she in despair about being left at Meddington after breaking-up, but her sheer, monumental ineptitude in the tender region of human relationships was an enduring misery. Would she ever learn? The vision of Jonathan's bleak, desperate embarrassment seared her. To have exposed him to her hysteria in front of his friends like that was unforgivable, and yet she had not foreseen the obvious when she had run after him. She wept, hot with shame.

She could see Jane Reeves in such a predicament being cool and tragic and heart-melting, with everyone sympathetic and admiring. Why couldn't she *learn*? God knows, she had had enough experience of embarrassing and unfortunate situations in the last couple of years to have at least learned the virtues of mere silence . . . but then Jane had said silence was inhibiting; one shouldn't bottle up one's innermost feelings. One must put out feelers, searching for response, for meaningful relationship. But she had put out bloody tentacles like an octopus and strangled Meredith almost to death.

She had felt in the past that life had come to a low

ebb, but never quite so low as this. Even when Robin had died. After all, Robin had been a dream, and one eventually woke up from dreams, but Jonathan wasn't a dream, and would reappear in the flesh in two days' time and no doubt go red as a pillar-box when he set eyes on her again. She had only been driven to approach him because she had sensed in him, somewhere under his reserve, an essential understanding of her loneliness. In a strange way, he was a lone person too, although highly regarded by just about everybody. Everybody liked him, yet he was close to no one. And having that ghastly Ashworth to share a study with ... it was like being on his own, for there was no common ground between them. She sensed that he wanted Ashworth because it made it as good as being on his own. Perhaps that was what attracted her to him: his forbearance with really horrible people. She and Ashworth were on a par, and he suffered them both without being unkind. Perhaps, following that logic, she had something in common with Ashworth? He had no friends either.

She couldn't picture things ever coming right for her, the way she was. There didn't seem to be any future at all. It didn't really matter, after all, whether her mother came later or sooner, as she didn't want to go home with her anyway. What had come as such a blow was her mother's complete unawareness of her daughter's life; she had forgotten – if she had ever known – that schools broke up for the summer holidays in July. When she wrote (seldom) she didn't even get the school's address right. She only wrote about her concerts, which Iris didn't want to read about. Iris, with a fresh outburst of self-pity, didn't understand why, out of all the millions of mothers in the world, she had to get one without that pre-requisite of ninety-nine per cent of the mother-race: a natural concern for its young. And, having got it, why God hadn't endowed her with an antidote in the way of a thick skin and an aggressive manner. She did not possess a single characteristic on the side of the angels;

her character was entirely made up of the flaws of the human temperament. Her report could well read: 'Iris is weak, tactless, intemperate, unperceptive and stupid.' All of them passive flaws, to be true – but even that could be a flaw in itself. Perhaps better to be actively rude, bad-tempered, unkind, self-righteous and stupid. At least one would feel better about the whole thing.

Jane came to look for her eventually, but was not exactly helpful.

'God, Iris, you do look a mess! You must pull yourself together. It's not the end of the world, staying on at school for an extra day or two. You won't be the only one.'

'It's not that, on its own. It's all sorts of things.'

'Giving Meredith ten fits in front of Murphy and co.?' Jane's voice was full of amusement, completely without sympathy. Iris did not reply.

'I can't think what possessed you! In front of Mr Hugo too. He was goggle-eyed. And poor Meredith obviously wanted the ground to swallow him up, poor devil. Do you fancy him?'

'No.'

'Parsons says he's going to be head boy, probably. I suppose he's that sort.'

'What sort?'

'Oh, you know, all the virtues. Pure and British and upstanding. Old-fashioned. Reliable, brave, handsome and polite.'

Iris had never thought of Meredith in that light.

'You make all those virtues sound like defects, the way you say them,' she pointed out.

'Do I?'

'What virtues do you prefer?'

Jane was surprised to hear Iris take the initiative. Iris was so far gone in self-contempt that she felt she had nothing to lose any more. She continued, 'I can guess without your telling me. You like them sexy, smart, sharp, witty, tall, dark and handsome.'

'Hm. You make that sound like a list of defects too.'

'It's the whole person you should like, because of a sort of understanding, not all the characteristics separately.'

"How would you know?"

Iris started to cry again.

'It is Meredith, isn't it?' Jane said.

'It's me,' Iris howled.

'Oh, do pack it in, Iris,' Jane said irritably. 'You are bloody hopeless.'

'I know, I know. That's what I'm crying about.'

'Oh, cripes.' Jane sat down on the bed and pulled a packet of cigarettes out of her handbag. 'Do shut up. Have a fag.'

'No.'

Jane lit one. 'Parsons says Meredith's in love with Mr Hugo.'

'Whatever do you mean?'

'The old-fashioned sort – you know, pure and virtuous, like nineteen-thirties schoolgirls having a crush on the games mistress. It's rather touching . . . somebody you admire very much.'

'How does Parsons know?'

'Oh, he just guesses. It's not a thing anybody *talks* about. It doesn't mean you're gay or anything. I mean, I know Meredith's got a girl-friend at home, because my cousin lives near them and she tells me. She's called Melissa Jones – Meredith's girl-friend, I mean. When he was in hospital over that shooting thing she used to visit him, and then he started to take her out. She met him at a point-to-point. They were both riding in it, and Melissa said he overtook her and after that she chased him all the way, even after it was over. She's a bit of a laugh, Melissa.'

Iris was silent, trying to picture this pushy Melissa. It didn't really help to know that Meredith had a girl-friend at home, somehow. It didn't cheer her up or anything. It only proved that perhaps Meredith wasn't such a loner after all. It just left her and Ashworth.

By the following evening, when the minibus was about due back from Wales, Iris went to see Ashworth. She was curious, and didn't care much what anybody thought, having sunk so low in the general estimation. Her self-respect was non-existent, her spirits at rock-bottom. It had rained heavily all day and the great Meddington trees were flinging their sodden heads sullenly against a thunderous, plumpurple sky. Everyone was packing, dragging heavy trunks along the corridors, and larking about. The lights were on, giving an eerie effect, and there was a smell of damp and old plimsolls and weary plaster. She moved slowly down the corridor, giving way to boys with large suitcases and one of the maids with a laundry basket, stepping over piles of cricket bats and pads, until she came to the study shared by Meredith and Ashworth. The door was open. Ashworth was emptying his cupboard.

Iris said, 'Oh, I thought Meredith was back.'

Ashworth gave her a malicious smile and said, 'You can't want to see him more badly than I do.'

'Do you know what time they're due?'

'They're back. The bus is down at Hugo's. You can see it out of the window.'

Iris went and had a look. She felt very nervous, seeing it, at confronting Meredith again, but her rock-bottom feeling compelled her to see it out. It was all so bad now, that it could – surely? – only improve. The thought of being left behind, after all this clatter and excitement had departed, was unbearable.

'You can wait, if you like,' Ashworth said. Iris was slightly surprised by the invitation and had a really dreadful feeling that it was extended out of malice, to annoy Meredith. Why else? Ashworth, like just about everybody in the whole school, knew how she had burst into tears on Meredith's neck. She sat down on one of the beds. She dreaded seeing Meredith come in, but there wasn't anything, the way things were, that she didn't dread in the immediate future. She just had to go through with it.

'Why do you want to see him so badly?' she asked.

Ashworth, packing books into a suitcase, did not reply at once. But when he had finished he said, 'He didn't say anything to you, about Hugo?'

'No. Why? What should he have said about Hugo?'

Ashworth, having bottled it up for so long, his mind-blowing secret, the news that would stop the whole school dead in its tracks, opened his mouth, shut it, and coloured up with violent emotion. Iris, thinking it was something to do with what Jane had said, waited with trepidation, intensely curious.

'He knows it's true, but he wants to keep it all hushed up – because it's Hugo – and he knows if he keeps me shut up until tomorrow – breaking-up, and everybody going home – then it'll all be all right, and Hugo will get away with it. But it's not *fair*!' Ashworth started throwing more books out of his cupboard on to his bed in a great rage. 'Just because it's bloody Hugo! He wouldn't care if it was Fletcher or Morris or anbody – else. You wait till he turns up – I'm going to tell him, I'm going to let him have it. I *shall* tell Armstrong, whatever he says.'

'Tell him what?'

'That Hugo murdered Robin. He didn't commit suicide. Hugo killed him. And Meredith knows it! Why should it be kept quiet, just because Meredith thinks Hugo's God and doesn't want anyone to know? It's not fair!'

'That Hugo *what*?'

'Hugo murdered Robin, threw him in. He was down there that night, late. Meredith saw him. He admits it. He knows it's true, but he won't let me tell anybody!'

'Hugo murdered Robin?'

'Yes. The suicide note was a fake.'

Iris stood up. Her mind blanked out. Seeing Ashworth, she saw Robin's face as she remembered it that time in the classroom, intensely sad and beautiful in her vision, and she saw it as a reflection of her own misery, ill-used, unloved and misunderstood. A great rage against the winners, the Hugos and head boys of the world, rose up in her like a storm. She shook from head to foot, like the tossing elms beyond the windows, and ran. Ashworth stared after her, shaken himself, more by having spilt the momentous secret than by her reaction to it. He was still staring when Jonathan came in.

Jonathan sat down on his bed, dumping his rucksack, and leaned back wearily against the windowsill. Coming back was awful – about twenty hours to get through, somehow, before his parents came for him tomorrow. It was all going to start now. He no longer knew how to handle the situation – if he had ever known from the start. No doubt Ashworth would give him a lead.

Ashworth was looking very peculiar.

'Did you see Iris?' he asked.

'No, thank God. Why?' Even talking about Iris would be better than about Hugo.

'She was here, waiting for you. I told her about Hugo and Robin.'

'You *what*?' Jonathan leapt up off the bed as if dynamited. 'You told *Iris*! Why Iris, for God's sake? You must be demented. Where is she?'

'She tore off like a mad thing.'

'She *is* a mad thing, imbecile! Where's she gone?'

'Search me. I thought she'd have passed you.'

'Why did you tell her? Why *her*? Have you told anybody else?'

'No.'

'What possessed you? Armstrong perhaps – but a lunatic like her! They all said she was gone on Robin. She'll do her nut, hearing you say that – look, I'll have to go and find her, before she does any damage. We

115

don't want it coming from *her*, Ashworth – Jeez, Ashworth, what possessed you? If you're still set on telling – I promise you, tomorrow, we'll go to Armstrong, after dismissal. It's true. I know now it's true. Does that satisfy you for the time being? But just sit on it a bit longer. I must find that girl.'

'She's there.' Ashworth nodded out of the window. Iris was running across the lawn towards the river, hair and draperies wild in the wind. It was nearly dark. A light was shining on the houseboat, twinkling through the tossing willows. 'She's going to the houseboat.'

Jonathan ran. There was no time to lose. Was she going to the houseboat? He had a much darker supposition than that, knowing her troubles and her state of mind. He tore down the stairs three at a time, leaping over the trunks and suitcases piled in the hall. The bell was ringing for junior bedtime and low rumbles of thunder from the black sky over Thornhill made a bass accompaniment, extremely suitable for the general mood. Jonathan couldn't believe it was happening, that perhaps he was still in the clutch of this dreadful mood which wouldn't believe the obvious, that just couldn't *accept* . . . Bursting out through the swing doors into the eerie, tremulous dusk, the sky quivering with distant lightning, the shaved lawns, electric-green, unreal, unrolling to that terrifying river, Jonathan knew that he should stop and get help, but it was all too late. Everything now was out of control. By the time he had explained, even found the right people to explain to, Iris would be gone the same way as Robin. Hot gusts of wind swept the lawns, bowling leaves and twigs and sodden sweet-papers, even a wire litter basket. Meddington blazed in the dark behind him like the sinking Titanic, unaware of danger. But Jonathan saw incredible dangers, and himself heading for them fast. He had a genius for getting himself into difficulties. McNair his friend at home had remarked on it once during one of his hospital visits.

Iris had disappeared amongst the willows. Jonathan burst his way through the long grass on to the bank, and ran along the path, ducking and cursing at the willows, bent and howling and whipping at him in the wind. The river was brimming with the rain, running high and hard, deceptively smooth. The water-flags were drowned and bent and their broken flowers swirled like stars, and debris on the surface was moving as fast as he could run.

He stopped and bawled into the wind: 'Iris! Iris! Don't – !'

But she was gone, almost as if spurred by his voice. He saw her jump and then blossom on the water like an opening water-lily, all her pale dress streaming and her long white arms upraised like reeds. The water seemed to eat her up, twist her over, take all her white petals and leave only sparks of phosphorescence. Then she surfaced again, and screamed. It was terrible.

Jonathan sped. In her scream he heard pure animal despair, not for living, but for dying. It was worse now, a hundred times, than it could ever have been before. There was no choice for him. Even while he was recalling with piercing clarity his conversation with Hugo concerning his life-saving abilities, he was doing a racing dive from the bank. The water was cold and fierce and unmanageable: he knew it instantly, feeling its power take him up like a living hand and bear him off like a little piece of flotsam. He fought to keep Iris in view and struck out for her without wasting time, knowing that if she went under again he would never trace her. Swimming with the current seemed ineffectual, but did in fact close the gap between them. It was only when he was within hailing distance that he realized that his troubles hadn't yet started, for Iris – it was painfully obvious – was going to be a classic example of the panicking victim. She could obviously swim enough to keep herself afloat and was now desperate to be saved, and her desperation would no doubt involve him in the drowning man's grasp – a situation practised with considerable gusto during lessons in the pool, but in no conceivable way comparable to the real thing. This was the real thing with a vengeance. Having come so far blindly and instinctively, Jonathan, in those last moments before closing with Iris, knew the terrible seriousness of his predicament. Instinct was now telling him that self-preservation should be governing his actions, but the moment had come, yet again, for the intellect to take over.

The idea was to approach the victim from behind. He knew that. But where was behind, in this black, turbulent frothing of current and screaming and flailing arms and whipping wet hair? Iris seemed to be going round like a top, and the current was twisting him off course too. It was just a matter of closing and hoping for the best. He saw her white face, demented, streaked with green weed, got a handful of her dress, pulled, tried to brake with his legs. The next moment he was under, with his neck in a vice-like grip. Hugo had been right about his chances . . . He fought and kicked, got a mouthful of air at intervals, swore at her, swallowed half the river . . . Her hands screwed his flesh; her bony knees gored him like bull's horns. She was trying to save herself, holding on to him out of fear of drowning; she even gasped it out, when he was far beyond mere conversation: 'Save me! Save me!' He was enraged at the irony of it: so close to being drowned himself, when nobody wanted it at all, not even her, though she had jumped in. Despair drove him. He pushed his hand into her face and forced it under. Her hands clawed at him, ripping off streamers of skin. He kicked her, desperate to sap her extraordinary strength, kept pushing her down until, at last, the fight went out of her. It wasn't according to the book. He thought he'd drowned her. He turned on to his back and heaved her after him by her hair, getting her body resting on his, her face up to the sky. The current took them, swirling in a nightmare

118

of weeds and hair and clammy cheesecloth, wrapping his legs and his face and his senses. He was scared rigid, unable to control the situation at all, not knowing where he was or what he was doing, only keeping a grip on the limp bundle and his face from going under. 'But it won't do,' he thought stupidly. 'I've got to do more.' There was a weir lower down, where Robinson had got hung up, but the river was in flood now and they would go over into the crashing foam beyond and stand no chance.

He tried to think of the topography of the river, its bends and islands, the best place to try and land, but his brain was too occupied with not sinking. Iris was like a great saturated parachute smothering him, tangling him. Her hair was all in his mouth and eyes. He didn't think they stood a chance and he hadn't any strength left for fighting. He was filled with anger and self-pity. 'What a bloody way to go,' he kept thinking, when even *she* hadn't intended it, and the weight of her pulled and dragged at him. He couldn't do anything. He was so tired. All his fine intentions were turned to spume, washing round him, his body spread-eagled and revolving in the current. 'I shall let her go,' he resolved, and something hard jabbed the back of his neck, bringing progress up sharp. There was mud and roots under the water, and trees black overhead, leaves brushing his face.

He clutched at the trailing branches with one hand, felt himself pulled and bumped by the current, clawed at earth and tearing grass as it slipped past. There was an alder tree leaning out, thin and ill-rooted. He caught it with one arm, hooked himself on and clutched at Iris with his other hand, his legs, his teeth, frantic she was going to slip out of his grasp. The current pushed her up hard against him. The alder swayed and tore and Jonathan shoved Iris at the bank with all his strength, straining until he all but passed out. She was like a bale of sodden straw, spent, saturated. He saw her fingers

open out on the grass like starfish, white claws
scratching for hold. He got his feet at her and pushed
and kicked her. The water boiled past. She was washed
up, moaning, choking, sobbing. Jonathan, spent, had
nothing left for himself at all, only his hands round the
alder and his body streamed out in the current, utterly
exhausted. It was all lunatic, a nightmare beyond
anything he could have imagined.

'The tree will come out and I shall go with it,' he
thought. 'I can't, I *can't* do any more ...' He was tired
to death. He locked his fingers round the bark, shut his
eyes.

He opened them when someone shouted. He couldn't
believe it. There was a rowing boat coming down fast
towards him on the current, someone back-peddling
with the oars to slow down.

'Here!' he croaked out.

The boat cannoned into the bank just upstream of
him, bounced off and scraped into the bowed head of
the alder tree. The figure reached out and caught the
branches, pulling the oars in sharply, moving very neatly and accurately in the emergency. He held on, and the
dinghy slewed sideways onto the current, but was
caught by the tree. The water boiled up along its side,
all but going over. The man in it lifted some branches to
allow the dinghy to stream bows on, and wrapped the
painter over the trunk to hold it, moving delicately, the
operation very tricky. Jonathan knew who it was by the
sheer efficiency of the operation. He wasn't saved after
all. He was back on the top of the climb, the death-drop
yawning, the same eyes regarding him. Hugo was really
in the clear this time. To drop the oar on his locked
fingers, cast him back into the current, and pull Iris in
after him ... Jonathan could see it all, even to his
obituary:' ... gave his life in a vain attempt to save a
drowning girl.'

'You nearly managed it,' Hugo said. 'I underestimated
you. Well done.'

'Don't –' It wasn't *fair*! Just what he had thought before. He hardly had the power any longer to hold his mouth clear of the water, let alone argue.

'What possessed her? I saw her go. I was going to the houseboat. I saw it all.'

'Ashworth told her –' Jonathan said. It was his only chance. He lifted up his head, feeling great sobs rending him at the way things had turned out – after all – when he had nearly, so nearly . . . 'Ashworth knows!' he sobbed out. He wanted to say, 'You can't get away with it, even if you drown us both now, because Ashworth will never let it rest. Ashworth is far more dangerous than I am, because he wants everyone to know, and I never wanted it. I would have covered up for you. Would, even now, if you give me the chance.' But he couldn't say any more, too spent, shuddering, his voice drowned out with the pure indignation of having to die for his pains, after everything. He wouldn't wait for Hugo. He would let go now. His fingers came apart. He went under.

Hugo lunged for him. He caught him by the hair and held on. Jonathan threshed out, too terrified to think, hit the dinghy transom and reached up. Hugo hauled. He got him under one arm and heaved wildly. Jonathan, full of water and unable to breathe, clutched as Iris had clutched, at anything, at Hugo, the dinghy, the branches, frantic. But the transom held him, once he had got his arms over, and Hugo held him by the hands to stop him sliding back, until he had choked the water up and found air again. Then Hugo let go of one hand, still holding the other, unwound the dinghy painter and clawed the dinghy through the branches to the bank. Jonathan felt the hard ground against his body and grasped the reeds and the grasses, digging his fingernails into the earth. Hugo clambered out, made the dinghy fast and came to his aid, hauling him bodily up the bank. Jonathan lay on his side, his head buried in the curve of his arm, unable to say anything. His breath

121

seemed to be coming in great shuddering sobs, wracking his whole body. He was aware of being alive, when he had expected to be dead, but was unaware of how to cope with being alive any longer.

'It's O.K., Meredith.' Hugo was kneeling beside him. Jonathan couldn't see his expression, but his voice was gentle, reassuring. 'It's all right now.'

Was it? Jonathan got his breathing under control, but not his shivering. He couldn't stop shivering.

'Iris?'

'She's all right.'

Everyone was all right. That's what Hugo said. Alive, he meant. Everyone was alive. But all right, Jonathan thought, was a different matter altogether. He couldn't see the next move at all.

But Hugo was taking over.

'We must sort out that idiot girl,' he said. 'When you've got your strength back we'll get her in the dinghy and take her back to my house. She seems to be in a state of shock.'

She wasn't the only one, Jonathan decided.

He couldn't move yet, Iris or no Iris. She had done for him. He rolled over, propped himself on his elbows, groaned. He felt sick. His ears were full of the rushing of the water; the trees grated and scraped on each other overhead and the wind rattled the leaves. Earth and leaves were stuck to his wet face, grass and earth in his mouth. He wiped his face, the drops running down off his hair. He didn't want to think about anything. But Hugo was right beside him, watching him. They were alone together, exposed, waiting, more vulnerable, both of them, than they had ever been before. It was no good avoiding it any more. If he could have moved then, scrambled to his feet, Jonathan would have done so. But it was no good.

'What are you going to do?' he asked Hugo.

'More to the point, what are you?' Hugo said.

'I can fix Ashworth. And Iris. There's nobody else.'

'Are you sure you can?'

'Yes.'

'I shall go away,' Hugo said. 'I shan't come back. I will make it as easy for you as I can. If, afterwards, you have to say what you know, I shall never blame you. Even now, if you have to. You owe me nothing.'

'No. It's only till tomorrow. It will be all right.' But he knew it wouldn't. Not for a long time. Not ever.

Hugo, sitting on the grass, tracing patterns on the earth with a twig, said, 'I can't explain to you what happened. It wouldn't be fair. It wasn't planned or intended. He deserved it, for all that he did to Patsy, for all that she suffered with him. He was laughing when he went over the side, laughing at us both. He never loved anyone but himself. I'm not sorry, I'm trying to say. I'm not excusing myself. I love Patsy. She is better off without him. In that respect I'm not sorry. Do you understand?'

'Yes, I knew. I guessed. I saw you together. But Ashworth found out and wanted to tell Mr Armstrong. He made me come to you with the book, else he would tell Armstrong. I didn't believe it, until then.'

'I'm sorry it was you,' Hugo said. 'Out of everybody.'

'Yes, I'm sorry too.'

'Oh, Christ,' Hugo said. 'I'm sorry.'

Jonathan knew what he meant, the inadequate word, repeated, too frail to cover the whole sorry tangle of death and misunderstanding and loving the wrong people. Hugo in that moment looked the same as he had that moment in the house when Jonathan had accused him, very young and not at all impressive, as tangled up as Jonathan felt himself. In that stripped way, so rare, he was closer than he had ever been. But it was no good any more, finished. It was another death in a way. Jonathan, seeing it, and knowing that Hugo saw it too, almost wished he was back under the water.

'Come on,' Hugo said. 'We must see to this girl.'

And it was over, back to the mechanics of living, getting Iris back, which was very difficult. She was conscious, but seemed completely unable to help herself, chalk-white and trembling like a leaf. They manhandled her into the dinghy and Hugo rowed across on the racing current. The water slicked past, curling across their bows like an animal snarling, lifting white lips, phosphorescent foam flicking in the darkness. Jonathan crouched down, not wanting to be reminded of the feel of it, more scared now at what he had done than when he was doing it. Hugo pulled strongly into the bank and caught at the reeds and shoved the boat hard home with an oar, then he made it fast with the painter and they lifted Iris out between them and hauled her up on the bank. They were well downstream of Hugo's cottage, and the school was out of sight. Hugo got Iris to her feet, and they got her between them, an arm around each of their necks and their arms crossed behind her back.

'Come on, gel,' Hugo said, kindly enough. 'It isn't far. Do your best.'

The long grass on the bank was flattened by the wind, moving as if animals were running through it. The willows streamed out, great crinolines of torn blue leaves reaching for them. They stumbled along, heads down, and Iris trailed between them, silent, weeping . . . how the girl cried, Jonathan thought, a reservoir of tears, but they were cold on his hand and she had no comfort at all, not even the comfort of making an end to it. Had she wished it . . . but no, she hadn't. There were sparks of hope in the darkness for them all, even for her.

It was a fantastic relief to get to the cottage and shut the door on the tearing wind. Hugo put on the light, but changed it quickly for a softer table-lamp, for there was, between the three of them, an animal instinct to avoid looking at each other: it was all so bare and difficult, too much having happened.

Hugo said, 'I'm going to pack up and go. It's best for everyone. I will have to go up to the school. I will tell

124

them Iris is staying with Patsy for the night, and I will see Ashworth, so no one will come looking for you. I take it you don't want anyone to know what's happened?'

'No!'

'You can see to Iris? I think she ought to get into a hot bath, and I'll get you some dry clothes. Can you manage?'

'Yes.'

'You can go back in the morning, early. In the morning, Meredith, you can say what you like. I shall be away.'

'I shan't say anything.'

'Iris might need some help.'

'I will see she is all right.'

'I will see you before I go.'

Hugo fetched Jonathan some clean jeans and a jersey and a towel, and lit the electric fire and started the bath running, then he went out. Jonathan felt completely washed up, not entirely sure he was still of sane mind. If he had been on his own he thought he would have flaked out there and then, wet clothes and all, but there was Iris. She was lying back in the armchair with her eyes shut, her face clear and white as marble, the blue veins showing like wreaths of smoke under the skin.

'Iris?'

Her eyes opened.

'Are you all right?'

They shut again. 'Yes.'

A pretty stupid question. He just meant not dead. It was first aid again, he realized, and he was all on his own now, with no help from anyone. But better that way, the only way to contain the extraordinary happenings of the day. Tomorrow they could all start again.

He went behind the armchair and stripped off, rubbed himself down and put on Hugo's clothes. He went upstairs and looked at the bathwater, waited for it until it was full enough, and turned off the taps. He went down for Iris.

What had he said about first aid? It was quite obvious now that Iris was beyond helping herself. But nothing any longer seemed out of place, getting her arm round his neck again and dragging her upstairs, sitting her on the edge of the bath and getting her undressed, undoing the clips of her bra, helping her into the water. There was no embarrassment in it, sitting on the edge of the bath while the warmth revived her, watching the marble-white faintly flushing to green-gold over her thin, lovely body, her hair netted out over her breasts, floating, her stone face softening.

'Don't cry,' he said gently.

'I'm sorry, I'm dreadfully sorry.'

'Don't be. Don't cry for it's coming out all right. It might have been far worse.'

'It can't ever really be quite so bad, after that.'

'No.' He wasn't quite so sure, for himself, whether the worst was over or not. But for her, very likely it was.

'You can come home with me tomorrow, until your mother's ready. My mother won't mind.'

She didn't cry again. He helped her get dried, and found a tracksuit of Hugo's for pyjamas, and put her into Hugo's bed and made her a cup of tea. She wound a towel round her head and lay propped on one elbow, drinking the tea. She looked quite normal again. Jonathan had no idea what time it was, but remembered something unpleasant about reading the lesson in the morning. He was too tired to have a bath himself, knowing he would fall asleep in it, but there wasn't another bed in the house, not even a sofa, so he got in with Iris, curling gratefully into the warm cave under the blankets, and slept instantly.

When Hugo came back he called out softly, got no reply, and went upstairs to investigate. They were both fast asleep, Iris's face turned into Jonathan's hair, half-hidden, her arm over his shoulders. He stood and watched them for a moment, strangely illuminated at intervals by the distant, receding lightning that danced through the mullioned window. His expression was one of great sadness.

'Meredith.'

Jonathan did not stir. Hugo put out a hand and shook his shoulder gently.

'Meredith.'

Jonathan's eyes opened and Hugo waited while he came to, the awakening bringing no joy. The eyes were definitely apprehensive.

'It's all right,' Hugo said. 'The intentions are friendly.'

'They weren't,' Jonathan said softly. 'Not on Cwm Silyn.'

'No.' Simply, no disclaimer.

Jonathan lay accepting the fact, watching Hugo's face, the mind not quite taking it in.

'I'm going now,' Hugo said, 'And I want you to know the truth. I wouldn't have woken you up for anything less.'

'About Robinson's death?'

'Yes. I wasn't going to tell you, but I've thought about it, and I want you to know because afterwards you might not think quite so badly about me. And on Cwm Silyn – well, I couldn't, it was simple enough. It would have been so convenient for me, so quick for you – quite the best way to go – but unfair. I don't want to grow old, but you might well prefer it. I couldn't do that to you.'

'Yes, I want to.'

'You've every chance, with me out of the way.' Hugo smiled faintly. 'Murder isn't so difficult, on a mountain or in deep water – I don't say I could cope with more sophisticated methods. But putting Robinson in that river – it was the best thing I ever did, Meredith. It was doing the human race a service, and Patsy in particular.'

'And you.'

'Because I love Patsy? Perhaps. But for what I do, it's

127

best not to love people too much. It comes between, doesn't it?'

For Hugo, perhaps, but Jonathan had never met anyone as self-contained as Hugo. It was true that he didn't seem to need anybody.

'Robinson was so deep in self-esteem, self-love, he was a swine. He couldn't have got by without Patsy to look after him, to make the decisions, to bolster him up, to protect him from real life, even to keep him, financially, before Meddington ill-advisedly took him on. And when she wanted to leave him – he was desperate. He resorted to everything – to humiliating her, beating her up, threatening suicide, even blackmail. He was going to tell Armstrong about our affair and get me the sack. I didn't kill him for that, because it was no threat to me – I would have left happily – I killed him because he was sitting there mocking her, reviling her, wallowing in self-pity. I felt so contemptuous. I just wanted to stop his mouth. So I did. No regrets.'

'No.'

'I threw him over. I knew he couldn't swim. I've never regretted it, not then nor since. I've seen far better men than him die. I'm quite used to it. Does it make sense to you now?'

'Yes.'

'But you – another matter altogether, I'm afraid. When I saw you in the river – I was desperate for you. I had gone through hellfire on the way home, thinking about it – the climb, I mean, and how I had been tempted. I thought I could never make amends. But then the opportunity came almost immediately – laid on by God Almighty, I suppose. Life is a very peculiar thing, Meredith.'

'I thought –'

'Yes, I know you did – God, Meredith, I would give anything not to have done all this to you!'

'It's all over now.'

'Only you have suffered through it.'

128

'And Robinson.'

'He's not worth tears.'

Talking of tears . . . Jonathan, his feelings stretched like elastic to what he sensed was breaking point, buried his head in the pillow, already wet from Iris's hair. Iris knew how to cry well enough; he must have learned a thing or two from her. He heard Hugo opening drawers and wardrobe doors, packing his clothes into a suitcase to go away. It was unbearable. Jonathan dared not surface, even when Hugo said, 'I'm going now.'

Hugo took the suitcases out to his car, and loaded all his climbing gear and the possessions he wanted, then came back into the living-room and looked round. It was bare and cold. An empty teapot and a bottle of milk stood on the table. He stood for a few seconds by the hearth, tracing a pattern in the dust on the mantelpiece with his finger, then he turned and picked up the climbing boots and ice-axe by the door, and went out.

Upstairs, hearing the door go, Jonathan turned in his sleep and said 'Hugo' out loud, but without gaining consciousness. It was six o'clock when he woke, and the sun was shining into the room.

CHAPTER
7

Iris, in fact, woke before Jonathan, the sun shining into her face, spearing her eyelids. She opened her eyes and saw the quaint cottage window, a swallow sitting on the carved eaves, and thick, bright leaves gleaming with moisture, very still, the sky clear and pale and shimmering, scoured by the storm. She remembered instantly what had happened, and where she was, and the fact that she was alive to appreciate what she was seeing was so mindbending a glory that she felt quite drained and petrified with gratitude. She did not move, feeling the warmth and comfort of the bed, the support of Jonathan's sprawled body beside her, watching the swallows flying backwards and forwards. Whatever had possessed her? Nothing in her life was that bad, was it? Not now, seeing the promise of the early morning, the optimism of the rising sun, not being alone, knowing she wasn't going to be left behind, it was fantastic. It was hard not to cry out of sheer gratitude. She lay staring at the moving shadows of the leaves on the old cracked ceiling, drinking in this extraordinary feeling of relief. Suppose she had really drowned herself last night, suppose those terrible moments of agonizing fear and regret had truly been her last moment on earth?

How could she possibly have . . . it seemed incredible now, that she could ever have thought it was that bad. If it hadn't been for Meredith . . .

She turned her head and looked at him still asleep beside her. It didn't mean anything, in the conventional sense, that she was in bed with a boy, but it seemed a very beautiful thing to her at that moment to be at rest, in companionable warmth and comfort, with the person who was responsible for her being alive at all. She had enough sense to know that he would not thank her if she was to convey these feelings to him, that if she tried she would only inflict upon him even worse embarrassments than she had already achieved so far, but she could think it, while he slept, without doing him any harm, for it was a part of her whole, lovely happiness. She loved him dearly, deeply, with this overwhelming sense of gratitude. It was nothing to do with sex at all, although it could well become so. It was to do with someone putting themselves to such trouble on her behalf, and not minding afterwards. She had never inflicted such rigours on another person before, nor been treated so gently. She lay looking at the sun playing over his face, hovering along his jawline, touching his pale eyelids and the profusion of curls springing over the white pillow. While she was watching, almost as if because she was watching, he opened his eyes. He looked at her and she saw the dazed sleep-stare clear to recognition. His eyes travelled over her face, went to the window beyond, and back again, and a look came into them of such pain and misery that she was startled. Remembering so vividly her own leaping happiness at seeing where she was a few moments before, and her own reaction to the window and the sun and the swallows, it did not seem possible that returning consciousness could bring such different emotions to him.

He sighed, and the look faded, and came back to her enquiringly, slightly nervous.

'Whatever would matron say?' he said.

Iris laughed.

He moved, groaned, 'Oh, how I ache!' – and lay back.

They lay without moving, speaking, until Iris turned her head and put her face against the bare shoulder and kissed it.

'Thank you, for me still being here. I didn't mean it.'

He looked at her and smiled, brought his arm up and put it so that her head rested on it. 'You could have fooled me.'

They lay there, both gazing at the ceiling, for some time. Then Jonathan said, 'Why did you?'

'I don't know. Perhaps I wouldn't have, if I hadn't known you were right behind me.'

'You mean it was all my fault?'

'It was Ashworth saying that. My mind sort of blew. I didn't think at all. It just seemed the last straw – about Robin.'

Jonathan said, 'It wasn't true, what Ashworth said. I must go and sort him out. He's got a bee in his bonnet, about Hugo doing Robin in. It's not true. You mustn't repeat it.'

'No, of course not. Not if it's not true. It doesn't sound likely at all.'

'No. It's just Ashworth. He's a bit touched.'

'Did Mr Hugo go last night? Or is he still here?'

'He's gone. He's on his way to Nepal, a plane to catch. I suppose we ought to make tracks too, if we're not to get found out. Do you feel O.K.?'

'Yes, perfectly.'

Jonathan moved his feet out on to the floor and sat there for a minute, as if to gather strength.

Iris said tentatively, 'Did you mean it – last night – about my going home with you?'

'Yes.'

Iris sat up, moved again almost to tears with relief and happiness. But she was very careful not to show it, determined not to put a foot wrong. She followed

Jonathan downstairs and out into the sunshine, silent, rejoicing: 'I will show him that I'm not stupid. I will be tactful and intelligent and kind and polite, and never cry again. I will make him admire me. I will make him love me. I shall never be stupid again.' The resolutions burst up inside her like fountains, and she walked along almost as if it was hard to keep her feet on the ground, her blonde mane cloaking Mr Hugo's maroon track-suit, shining in the sunlight.

Jonathan felt a great relief at parting from Iris, the urgent business of the day at hand. The rising bell hadn't yet gone, although a lot of the younger boys were larking about, the prospect of release having activated them earlier than usual. He went upstairs scowling, feeling stiff in every joint and delicate in the brain-box, acutely miserable, nervous, knocked sideways and longing for home. He longed for the peace and security of his own bedroom, with a lock on the door, where he could wind down and come to grips with what had hit him, accept it, relax, forget. Opt out. Hugo having admitted to murder, Hugo having intended to murder *him*! Hugo saying he was sorry – and about the truth of that there was no doubt at all. Jonathan knew he would never forget seeing Hugo's face in the extremity of his regret, the real emotion which he never showed ordinarily, Hugo off his pedestal, infinitely human and vulnerable, Hugo down to earth. It was all finished. He would never see him again, nor know the answers, nor speak to anybody of what had happened. Except Ashworth.

Ashworth was still asleep.

Jonathan looked down at him with contempt.

He went to his wardrobe and got out the only clothes still there, his best uniform, laid it on the bed, and went to the bathroom to get cleaned up. When he got back he got dressed and combed his hair and woke up Ashworth.

'Where've you been?' Ashworth scowled, coming up out of the blankets, blinking, like an animal out of its lair, eyes pink and bleary. 'What happened?'

'Nothing happened that I'm going to tell you.'

'A kid brought a message – said it was from you, that you wouldn't be back till morning. What happened to Iris?'

'She was O.K.'

'What are you going to do about Hugo? It was true – you admitted it last night. He did murder Robinson. We're going to Armstrong?' Ashworth began to emerge, shining and damp with anticipation, pleased with the day's prospect. 'You said –'

'I might have said it to you,' Jonathan said, 'but I shall never say it again, to you or Armstrong or anybody else.'

'But it's true – you said! You promised –'

'It might be true, but you won't get me to admit it. Hugo's gone away. You can't touch him. And no one will believe you. There's no evidence.''

Ashworth's expression changed, darkening first to suspicion, then anger. 'You won't come to Armstrong with me?'

'No.'

'You swine, Meredith! You back-sliding cheat! You promised, after you came home – you said –'

'It's all changed, Ashworth. Hugo's gone away and he won't come back. He's gone to Nepal. Nobody's going to bother to chase him out there on your word alone, so you might as well forget it.'

'He's gone because it's true, you mean? Run away – he knows he's been found out? Is that it?'

'I'm not telling you now, nor ever. You can draw your own conclusions.'

'It is true then.'

'If you like.'

Ashworth lay back, baffled and angry.

'You can't stop me telling what I know.'

'If it pleases you, no, I can't. But you know very little. If you don't get up now you'll miss breakfast.'

'Fletcher wants to see you before breakfast.'

'I'll go now then.'

'No, wait . . . you really are a swine, Meredith. What if I was to tell what I know? If Hugo's done a bunk it must be true, that he's guilty.'

Jonathan hesitated. Ashworth was persistent with the perseverance of a hunting animal, or a mole travelling down its tunnel. Jonathan was putting on his watch, a new gold digital watch that his father had given him 'for good conduct' after he had come out of hospital in the spring. He slipped his wrist out of the bracelet and handed it over.

'Will that keep you quiet?'

Ashworth's face changed, incredulous joy chasing away the resentment.

'You don't mean it!'

'I do, for shutting up.'

'Cripes, Meredith, I won't breathe a word! Cross my heart. I've forgotten already!'

Jonathan was confirmed in his hunch about Ashworth's motives: that his thirst to disclose the truth was due more to power-lust than to clearing his own guilt, to get a good person into trouble. He left the room, knowing he had won, but hurt by the cost. Certainly it was worth it, but it was going to be very awkward when his parents realized the watch was missing. He'd have to think up a good story. He was a rotten liar, having been brought up that way.

'Meredith!'

'Sir?' It was Fletcher, emerging from his study while he was in the act of raising his hand to knock on the door.

'Did you get my message – *before* breakfast?' The breakfast bell was ringing at that moment. 'I can't help thinking we've made a dreadful mistake, but the summons was to inform you, Meredith, that you're to be head boy next term.'

Jonathan felt as if Fletcher had jerked the carpet from under his feet. He felt his mouth drop open. On top of the watch, and considering his late experiences, it was almost more than he could take.

'You don't look pleased,' Fletcher truly commented. 'However that doesn't surprise me. I put your name forward against my better judgement, in the earnest hope that it will do you more good than the school. We can but live in hopes.'

Jonathan, aggrieved, walked with Fletcher down the wide staircase, lesser mortals standing on one side.

'It is what you need, Meredith, to draw you out of your shell. And I hope and trust that you will rise to the opportunity of serving your school in the way I know you are capable of, putting self aside.'

Jonathan expected to hear heavenly voices breaking into 'Land of Hope and Glory'. He wondered what was for breakfast.

'Yes, sir.'

'You have some very fine qualities. We want you to use them.'

'Yes, sir.'

Fletcher was not more specific, unfortunately, and left Jonathan curious, but too modest to enquire further.

'Where were you last night, by the way? You have a bad habit of not being around when wanted, which you will have to cure.'

Jonathan wasn't sure what to answer, pretty sure that 'in bed with Iris Webster' would not be in keeping with his new status.

'Er, clearing up, sir.' Which, after all, described the goings-on of the night before fairly accurately.

'Mr Simms wanted you to go through the lesson. You've remembered you're reading?'

'Yes, sir.'

'You should have reported to him. You go your own way far too much, Meredith, you know. We shall expect total reliability next year.'

Kippers, Jonathan thought, super –

'And a haircut while you're about it.'

No, he didn't want to do it, and would hate the ultimate responsibility of the post, being nailed to the side of authority, neither fish nor fowl, and having to make the right decisions about other people when he couldn't even make them for himself, but a little part of him took it as a compliment. It would please his parents, might make it easier about the watch, if he told them he was head boy first, and had lost the watch immediately afterwards. He would get a study to himself and, with luck, a decent mattress. Only a year to go anyway, the last lap. It would be bleak without Hugo. His eyes went automatically to the staff table, and the gap where Hugo should have been, and he didn't hear what Fletcher said as they parted. The smell of kippers turned his stomach, now that he was at the serving-table.

Miles behind with his packing, he was late into the hall for the breaking-up service, taking the reader's seat on the platform just as the Head was spreading his papers out at his table. Simms came up and hissed at him, 'I've marked the passage, Meredith – you really are too bad, not to have reported for a read-through! One expects better of a prefect.'

Shades of next year . . . Jonathan muttered his excuses, knowing that the passage was always marked on the opened page, and not having given it a thought. He had learned to read, at least, come the upper sixth, even if other things of importance seemed to escape him.

He sat through the familiar beginnings of the service, not listening, merely resting. He realized he felt tired to death, all ways, physically and mentally, too washed up even to think about what had happened. His mind felt as if it were far away, down a deep burrow. He leaned back on the hard chair, hearing meaningless words ricocheting round the complexities of the ornamental ceiling, watching calming sunlight washing the pale plaster. His condition was one of anaesthesia, numbing the dire disasters that lurked in his soul-regions, hopefully until the worst of the pain might have abated by the passage of time. This happened, he knew, though it was hard to believe. At the moment pure exhaustion wasn't a bad option.

Primed by darting fire from the eyes of Mr Simms from the row of staff, he got to his feet and crossed the platform to the lectern, timing his arrival at the exact moment the Head's voice finished whatever it was it had been saying. Ten out of ten for timing. He fixed his eyes on the passage required, covered in cellophane and marked as for an idiot in thick red marking felt. Underneath was written, 'Now turn to where blue marker is inserted and read on.' It was like an equestrian dressage test, with perhaps the same requirements: rhythm and accuracy. He prepared his biblical voice, shot a glance at Armstrong for the starting-bell, and proceeded.

'Lord, who shall dwell in thy tabernacle, or who shall rest upon thy holy hill? Even he that leadeth an uncorrupt life, and doeth the thing which is right, and speaketh the truth from his heart. He that hath used no deceit in his tongue, nor done evil to his neighbour, and hath not slandered his neighbour. He that setteth not by himself, but is lowly in his own eyes . . .'

It was as if his mind quite suddenly came out of its dream, fixing upon these words that his voice was delivering as if they themselves were inscribed in red marker each ten feet high.

'When I was in trouble, I called upon the Lord and he heard me. Deliver my soul, O Lord, from lying lips, and from a deceitful tongue . . .

'I will lift up mine eyes unto the hills, from whence

cometh my help. My help cometh even from the Lord, who hath made Heaven and earth . . . '

The words came up off the page and clobbered him in the face; he could not see what he was supposed to be reading. He heard his voice falter and felt panic taking over. His dressage horse was out of control and bolting round the ring. He put his hands up, as if to steady the dancing print, but the cellophane stuck to his suddenly sweaty fingers and moved off-course. He came to a complete stop. In that moment he thought, if the words were making the sense they seemed to be, there was nothing left but to do as he had been so recently advising the whole school: 'When I was in trouble I called upon the Lord . . . ' Jesus, help me! The sun-washed hall was full of a strange, beautiful silence, five hundred faces upturned in curious wonder, riveted by the silence far more than they had ever been impressed by the words. But the words, Jonathan thought, had been hand-picked by bloody Simms, as if he *knew*, marked up with malicious glee to grip his vocal chords in paralysis, to punish him for his lack of preparation. Panic at his plight had overcome the initial surge of emotion that had thrown him in the first place: this he could control, given time. He cleared his throat to break the silence and took a deep, quivering breath.

'The Lord himself is thy keeper . . . ' It didn't sound too peculiar, only breathless. He was dreadfully short of breath. He took it slowly, aiming at the back of the hall, desperate to wind up in composure. He was never going to live this down otherwise, as bad as the Iris episode, and even more public. If only the Lord would take on Iris . . . at the moment he was Iris's keeper, and would happily forgo the job.

He got to the end – unless the marker, having moved, was deceiving him – and made his retreat, glancing at Armstrong as he did so and receiving an extremely thoughtful glance in return. The hymn was announced, and he was able to recover under the blanket of the loud cheerful noise, aware now that he was trembling and feeling rather sick. Roll on, this eternal day, he prayed, I want to go home. The choir led out and seatings were rearranged for the prize-giving, during which Fletcher waylaid him on his way back to the sixth-form contingent and said, 'What afflicted you, Meredith?', suspicion overlaying a certain sympathy.

'Hay-fever, sir. I was going to sneeze.'

'You have great presence of mind. It will stand you in good stead next year.'

Jonathan thought about this remark, going back to his place, not thinking that it was meant as a compliment, the way it was said. No doubt Fletcher recognized 'the deceit in his tongue', but admired how promptly it was produced. It had surprised him too. He had to think about anything, really, than the feeling on the platform that had undone him, the truth of what was lying under this inertia of the brain, for he couldn't face it at all. He must be terribly careful to avoid thinking in the near future. Better to get gloomy by watching the onerous duties Parsons was performing, knowing it would be himself next year, than over the Hugo thing: showing the governors to their places, smiling at Lady Pemberton, aged ninety-nine or thereabouts, and picking up the handbag which had fallen under her chair, consulting with Armstrong about the order the cups were to be presented in – worst of all, he had the notes for his customary speech stuck in his top pocket: there was a horror to dwell on, to occupy the mind with perfectly, why ask for more? Jonathan sank lower in his seat.

Murphy said, 'What happened to you? I thought you were going to have a fit.'

'I had a vision. God smote me.'

'You've been working up to it – very odd, the last few days. Feel better for it?'

'I'll feel better when I get shot of this place.'

'Who won't? It gets you down after five years or so.'

When his mother came, Jonathan kissed her with an affection born of colossal relief. She was surprised, and looked at him curiously, on a level now, although she was tall. Jonathan decided to get it all over at once.

'I'm going to be head boy next year.'

'Really? I'm surprised! I thought you were one of these opters-out.'

'Well, perhaps that's why. Compulsory opting in. I'm not sure. No doubt Armstrong will tell you if you ask. I rather get that impression. Also, I've lost the watch Dad gave me.'

'Jonathan! How incredibly careless! How could you?'

'In Wales, I don't know where – well, if I did, it wouldn't be lost. I feel bad about it.' Bad about what he was saying too. He couldn't look her in her sharp eyes, and scuffled his toe in the gravel.

'Your father will be upset. It was intended to mean something, that watch, after all that happened, not just a casual gift.'

'I know.'

'It was worth a lot, and I don't mean necessarily the cost.'

'I'm sorry.' It had been worth a good deal in its departure too, the only consolation.

He pressed on, aware that he was pushing his luck. 'There's something else – it's a bit difficult. I hope you won't mind –' He glanced up warily, always slightly nervous of his mother ('And not the only one,' Fletcher might have added with sympathy): 'I've promised someone they can come home with me for a day or two. I didn't think it would put you out very much.'

'Oh. Well, you might have given me a bit of warning. But I don't mind, no. Who is he? Anyone I know?'

'No. It's a girl.' More gravel scrutinizing. 'She's stranded – her mother's got the dates wrong or something. And she's a bit desperate about being left and I – well, I was a bit sorry for her – I said –'

141

'Good heavens, Jonathan, a girl! Any more surprises? Are you fond of her?'

'No, it's not like that at all. You wait till you see her. She's a bit – er – peculiar, I suppose – but harmless. I'll go and tell her you're here.'

Introducing Iris to his mother, Jonathan wondered if his troubles might only just be starting, rather than ending. Iris was unexpectedly garbed in a severe dark dress of a brownish-purplish design, against which her hair, tied back, sprung out in a positively green, shining fan down her back. She smiled in a bright, shining way he had never seen before – shining was the only word he could think of, watching her, when up to now it had been all glooming and weeping . . . it made last night seem like a dream, or a nightmare, all that green hair wrapped round him like the very weeds under the water, and her wild despairing hands tearing at him – and now . . . Jonathan began to wonder whether it had ever happened, watching her – perhaps none of it . . . it was all in his head, hallucinations, brought on by pressure of work. What work? No. Not to start thinking like that. It was true all right.

His mother was obviously somewhat amazed by Iris, but perfectly cordial. They went back into school to get their luggage, and Jonathan said to Iris, 'Don't say anything about what happened, will you? Last night, I mean – you don't want anyone to know, do you?'

'No. But you ought to get some credit – what you did – my mother ought to give you a hundred pounds or something.'

'From what you said about her I should have thought the very opposite.'

Iris giggled. 'A hundred pounds for letting me sink?'

'Promise you won't say anything. Nor about what Ashworth said, that set you off. None of it was true.'

'All right, if you say so.'

They loaded the Rover and said the obligatory good-byes, and at last, the moment Jonathan had so longed for, they were driving away from Meddington down the long sweep·of gravel, past the deserted flint cottage by the edge of the pine-wood, through the deep-shaded belt of the boundary woodland where the thrushes were singing their afternoon songs and out into the open country. The blessed relief enfolded Jonathan with such balm that he lay back in his seat, shut his eyes and almost drifted into unconsciousness. It was as if he had just freed himself from a rucksack full of granite rocks.

'It is finished,' he thought. 'It is all over. It will be all right, given time.'

And the car slipped along the road to Thornhill, past the water-meadows where the cows were grazing and past the wide, snaking, beautiful river, which Jonathan could feel twisting and turning his body and closing over his head and pulling him down, and knew he would never forget.

Jonathan was never quite sure where one story in his life ended and another one started. He thought going home would put this one behind him, shutting the door of his room on the outside world, lying on his own bed in complete privacy and solitude and letting his mind wander over it at last. The last upheaval in his life had been resolved in this way during his convalescence in hospital, having time to think, away from people who probed. Boarding school was terrible for having nowhere alone. He always came home with a thirst for the peace of Ravenshall, but never so thirsty as this time, and never so grateful for haven. (Usually, quite soon, he got bored, but that was another thing altogether).

'You look tired, dear,' his mother said. 'I do hope it's from working too hard.'

He grinned and said nothing.

Iris was a new person, taking to Ravenshall as if to a native haunt, enchanted by its order and its beauty and the novelty of a country routine, taking even to Mrs Meredith which Jonathan found amazing.

'She's so unmusical,' she said to Jonathan. 'You can't imagine the relief.'

Mrs Webster, after a few phone calls, gratefully left Iris where she was, and Iris blossomed in her content, and took to gardening and long walks with the dogs, but not to horses, even after seeing Jonathan at it.

'I'm not brave enough.'

'It doesn't need bravery,' Jonathan said. 'Not for hacking. Any fool can do it.'

He rode a large bay race-horse called Florestan, and Iris wasn't convinced, and would not be persuaded. 'I'm very happy as I am.'

And Jonathan left her and rode on his own, and went on thinking about what he thought of as the Hugo thing. Whenever he was on his own he thought about it, about Hugo, the rock, being splintered by the tangle of events which he, Jonathan, had precipitated by his admiration, by merely being where he was at the wrong time, by trivial circumstance. His thinking resolved nothing, but he needed it, the never-ending circular trail curiously restful to the sore brain, dreaming the summer months away. It was his cure.

'Jonathan, you are spending your holiday in an extremely unproductive fashion to date,' his mother announced at breakfast. 'All this mooching about. I think you need organizing.'

'Oh, no! I need the rest.'

'You're not telling me you're overworked at that holiday home they choose to call a school?' his father enquired, rustling out from behind the *Daily Telegraph*. 'Something here will interest you. Another of your teachers – they kick the bucket like ninepins at that place. What d'you think of this? Anyone who takes you?'

He pushed the newspaper over to Jonathan, stabbing with his forefinger to a column of news on the front page. It was headed quite starkly, 'Charles Hugo killed in avalanche on Nuptse.'

Jonathan took it in without a word or a change of expression, still sawing the top off his boiled egg.

'Isn't that the fellow that takes you for maths? His name's on your report.'

'Yes.'

'That's it – you went to Wales with him?'

'Yes.'

'That's tough, eh! He was a fine fellow from all accounts.'

'Yes.'

But it was more than flesh and blood could manage, to eat a boiled egg. He pushed his chair back and went out of the room. His parents looked at the closed door with what Iris recognized as a sort of respectful acknowledgement of emotions better not discussed, pushed under the carpet in proper British fashion. She remembered what Jane had said. What Ashworth had said. What Jonathan had said about Ashworth. She remembered Hugo's kindness that night, the expression in Jonathan's eyes when he had woken up.

'Another cup of tea, Iris?' Mrs Meredith asked.

How extraordinary they were, Iris thought, like the old empire. No wonder Jonathan was as he was, all the things Jane had said about him as if they were insults, one of nature's head boys. Burdens were accepted, and carried alone, without complaint. Part of the tradition. Admirable? Daft? Daft, Iris decided, with a great surge of compassion for Jonathan. She, too, could not face her boiled egg. She put down her spoon, and the first tears since Meddington welled up and splashed down her cheeks.

'Oh, my dear,' said Mrs Meredith. 'It's a shock for you both. I'm so sorry.'

But Iris wasn't crying for Hugo. She was crying for Jonathan's old-fashioned virtues, and for herself, who loved him so, and for all the things that wouldn't happen for either of them, however much they wished it.

'Here, another cup of tea will make you feel better. Death by accident is always a great shock.'

'Better take one to Jonathan,' Mr Meredith said drily.

'No. Oh, no. You know Jonathan.'

Mr Meredith pushed his empty cup over and turned to the business pages.

Long afterwards, when all the thinking was over, Jonathan supposed it was better that way. For him, at least. Not for Hugo, aged twenty-seven – and, when scared, about ten years younger, the same as himself in fact. Jonathan knew what Hugo had looked like when the avalanche had closed over him. He might – who knows? – have been the only person who had ever seen Hugo look like that, Hugo of whom the obituary said: 'Charles Hugo was utterly fearless . . .' Jonathan wasn't so sure.

There were a lot of things he wasn't sure about, and never would be. Even the avalanche. Hugo had always said, 'The risk is as great as you make it.' Perhaps Hugo had pushed it a bit more than usual. By his own admittance such a death was 'quite the best way to go'. So be it, Jonathan thought, and an uncontrollable shudder went through him, remembering how it felt.

Two weeks after Hugo's death he received a letter from the leader of the expedition, enclosing a postcard addressed to him from Hugo, which had been found in Hugo's gear after the accident. The date on the postcard, a photograph of the Nuptse approach, was almost a month before the date of Hugo's death. Jonathan thought that perhaps Hugo, having written it, had decided against sending it off, or perhaps he had left it in his personal things for just such an eventuality. The message was brief. 'You would be in clover here, Meredith. Goodbye. CH.'

The covering letter said, 'Charles wasn't much of a

correspondent. I only ever knew him to send two or three postcards per expedition, so all the more reason for preserving this one. I understand you are one of his pupils at Meddington. What a privilege to have been taught by him, and what a pity you will never have the privilege again.' Words of a noble ring. 'And the privilege of being murdered by him . . . ' how very nearly true . . . but Jonathan shed tears over the postcard. It was worse than reading about the death in the newspaper. It truly was the end, inscribed by his own hand, and Jonathan knew that this time the story was closed. Jonathan stayed in his room playing records, and went for long rides on Florestan.

Ten days before he was due back at school he said to his mother, 'Do you see anything of Melissa around these days? I think I'll give her a ring.'

'Melissa Jones?' There was no rapture in Mrs Meredith's voice. 'Why not? Hibernation over?'

Jonathan looked surprised, then grinned. 'Could be.' He looked at Iris. 'It's been terribly dull, this holiday for Iris.'

His mother rolled her eyes and murmured, 'God grant me strength! Whose fault was that?'

'We needed a rest,' Jonathan said. 'Didn't we?' he asked Iris. 'It's very gruelling at Meddington.'

'Yes, it's awful.'

'It'll be all right next term,' Jonathan said to her. He opened his eyes very wide and saw Iris brown and freckled, her hair in a long plait, wearing jeans and a shirt. He suddenly realized all the other things he ought to have been thinking about, all the quite normal, everyday problems of life, like Iris (in capital letters) and making some new speakers for his stereo, and seeing if Florestan might be turned into an event horse, and getting some tickets for that gig at the Roundhouse that Parsons had mentioned – probably been and gone by now –

'I thought we were going to Ireland?'

'On Tuesday, dear.'

'Iris too?'

'Yes. Her mother's abroad. And we shall be happy to take her.'

'Oh, jeez,' he thought but didn't say it. He still had problems all right. He could tell by the way she looked at him. He had never noticed before. How extraordinary! Driving lessons was the other thing, to polish him up for the test. But he hadn't even put in for it yet and the waiting list . . . oh, blast.

'Have you got a form for taking the driving test?' he asked his mother.

'I've already passed. Why should I have?'

'But I want to – I must get one. How much does it cost? Or do you ring them up or something?'

'You are a very odd boy,' his mother said, never having quite come to terms with it.

'Bear with it. I'll be eighteen in no time. One day you'll be glad you knew me.'

'I do hope so.'

Meanwhile, he thought, drive a steady course making all the right signals, anticipating danger, proceeding only when safe to do so. He would be an exemplary head boy and stun them all.

'You don't really mind going back, do you?' he asked Iris.

'Not really, now. It's all tons better, coming here.'

She had actually put on weight, the angularities rounded out. Her face no longer had that gaunt look any more, and the froggy-green effect had vanished. Jonathan thought suddenly that she seemed a whole lot easier to live with than heretofore. Perhaps Ireland would be quite nice, rambling across the empty beaches with this peculiar girl.

Nevertheless, he rang up Melissa while Iris was getting some lettuces out of the garden for lunch.

'Good heavens, you!' she said and giggled.

'What's so funny? Will you come out with me to-night?'

'No, I can't. I've got engaged to Clive Howarth.'

'Oh.' Not much to say to that. 'Oh well. Hm. I thought – oh, well.'

'What did you think?'

'You liked me, once.'

'Yes, ever so, but you're never there, are you?'

'And Clive is? Must be, to woo you that fast. What's he like?'

'Lovely. Very rich, like you, but older. Twenty-seven.'

Like Hugo.

Poor Hugo.

'I hope you'll be very happy.'

She giggled again. 'Why don't you come over and say it in person? There's no rules against it. Tuesday?'

'I'm going to Ireland on Tuesday.'

'Oh, lucky old you. Never mind. I shall always love you like a friend, Jonathan. You're too young, that's all. Have a lovely time.'

'And you.'

He rang off, not quite sure whether to be amused or indignant. Whichever way, he couldn't honestly say it hurt. Nothing hurt very much any longer, which was a great relief. He couldn't even think of anything to worry about very much either, apart from being head boy, and Iris, and both those were within his scope, with normal luck.

There would be time to inquire about a driving test before lunch. He reached for the telephone book and started to search for the number, and when Iris came back he was talking dates and costs, nothing to do with Melissa at all. She took the lettuces over to the sink, and started to wash them, smiling.

About the Author

K. M. Peyton has written books since she was a young child and her tenth attempt was published while she was still at school, aged sixteen. She studied painting at art school, ran away from home to get married and, with her husband – a fellow student, worked her way across Europe for a year. On her return, she taught art for three years at Northampton Art School and then went to Canada, where she worked until she and her husband had enough money to travel round Canada, returning home through the States.

K. M. Peyton's interests include horses, sailing and music. The Peytons live in Essex and sail mainly in east coast waters, with trips abroad in the summer. They have two daughters.

K. M. Peyton has several times been a runner-up for the Carnegie Medal and in 1969 was awarded the Medal for *The Edge of the Cloud*. In 1970 she received the Guardian Children's Book Prize for her *Flambards* trilogy.

Other Puffins by K. M. Peyton

FLAMBARDS
THE EDGE OF THE CLOUD
FLAMBARDS IN SUMMER

Twelve-year-old orphan Christina is sent to live with her Uncle Russell and his two sons in their old country house, Flambards. It is a strange, unruly household that Christina grows up in during those years before the First World War: one she comes to love, hate and be inextricably bound up with.

Horses and early flying machines mix in this unforgettable trilogy with romance, love, cruelty and drama.

PROVE YOURSELF A HERO

One can never prepare to be kidnapped; to anticipate the terror, exhaustion and violence; or to understand the disorientation and unbalance that accompanies the return to freedom – if one is lucky. Jonathan Meredith's disappearance, apart from anything else, was annoying. It cost a half a million pounds and mucked up a lot of arrangements – and for Jonathan things would never be the same again.

Some other titles in this series

EMPTY WORLD
John Christopher

Neil Miller is alone after the death of his family in an accident. So when a virulent plague sweeps across the world, dealing death to all it touches, Neil has a double battle for survival: not just for the physical necessities of life, but with the subtle pressures of fear and loneliness. A chilling portrait of a world where a nightmare has come true.

TULKU
Peter Dickinson

Escape from massacre, journey through bandit lands, encounters with strange Tibetan powers – and beneath the adventures are layers of ideas and insight. Winner of both the Carnegie and Whitbread Awards for 1979.

SURVIVAL
Russell Evans

High tension adventure of a Russian political prisoner on the run in the midst of an Arctic winter.

A QUEST FOR ORION
Rosemary Harris

Europe overrun by neo-Stalinists is the setting for this compelling depiction of resistance to tyranny and of the improvisation and endurance needed in a fragmented world.

MISCHLING, SECOND DEGREE
Ilse Koehn

Ilse was a Mischling, a child of mixed race – a dangerous birthright in Nazi Germany. The perils of an outsider in the Hitler Youth and in girls' military camps make this a vivid and fascinating true story.

THE TWELFTH DAY OF JULY
ACROSS THE BARRICADES
INTO EXILE
A PROPER PLACE
HOSTAGES TO FORTUNE
Joan Lingard

A series of novels about modern Belfast which highlight the problems there, in the story of Protestant Sadie and Catholic Kevin, which even an 'escape' to England fails to solve.

THE ENNEAD
Jan Mark

A vivid and compelling story about Euterpe, the third planet in a system of nine known as the Ennead, where scheming and bribery are needed to survive.

THE DEVIL ON THE ROAD
Robert Westall

John Webster took no chances with his Triumph Tiger-Cub but he thought he was playing games with Chance, like tossing a coin to see which road to follow. But maybe Chance was playing games with him?

Puffin Plus non-fiction

KNOW YOUR BODY
Dorothy Baldwin

A witty, helpful guide to matters of health for young people. A book for browsing through, laid out in alphabetical order, and designed to help understand the mental and physical changes which occur during the teens.

THE MOTORCYCLING BOOK
John Dyson

Buying a bike, driving safely, knowing how it works . . . virtually everything an inexperienced rider needs to know about motorcycles and mopeds is brought together in this comprehensive guide. Follow its advice and you will get the best value from owning and riding a two-wheeler.

WHY DIDN'T THEY TELL THE HORSES?
Christine McKenna

Actress Christine McKenna had never been on a horse in her life, apart from an endearing donkey on the beach at the age of three. So when she landed the star role of the hunting and riding Christina in the TV serial *Flambards*, some incredible experiences were ahead of her. This is the good-natured, frequently hilarious story of one diminutive actress and her relationship with a host of horses . . . some co-operative, some disdainful, and many stars in their own right.

SNAP!
Christopher Wright

Black and white or colour, still-life or action shot, scenery or family group, this book will help you make your photographs turn out as you intended. Starting with straightforward explanations of seven different types of camera, there is lots of sensible information about choosing films, settings and apertures, and sound advice on how to tackle your first subjects. A comprehensive, highly illustrated handbook that will prove invaluable to every beginner.

SOME PENGUIN BOOKS YOU MIGHT ENJOY

THE CRIME AT BLACK DUDLEY
Margery Allingham

THE DAY IT RAINED FOREVER
Ray Bradbury

FAREWELL MY LOVELY
Raymond Chandler

TALES OF THE UNEXPECTED
Roald Dahl

THE FIRST OF MIDNIGHT
Marjorie Darke

THE MILLSTONE
Margaret Drabble

WHITE EAGLES OVER SERBIA
Lawrence Durrell

BRIGHTON ROCK
Graham Greene

HOW TO BE AN ALIEN
George Mikes

GIRL WITH GREEN EYES
Edna O'Brien

CRY, THE BELOVED COUNTRY
Alan Paton

WHAT ABOUT TOMORROW
Ivan Southall

THE PICTURE PALACE
Paul Theroux

THE DAUGHTER OF TIME
Josephine Tey

WEB
John Wyndham